"We'll go on another adventure tomorrow," Trey promised his son.

Little Billy looked at Jo. "I want Jo to come, too."

"Oh, Billy," she protested, "I can't—"

"Why in tarnation not?" Trey interrupted. He was all confidence and cocksure cowboy. But his droll smile warmed his eyes with teasing and sent heat coiling through Jo's limbs.

And there was enticement in his voice as he added, "Won't you give us your tomorrow, Jo?"

"Please…" a small voice cajoled.

If Trey had simply insisted, Jo could have stood her ground.

But how could she ignore the guileless plea of a five-year-old?

And how could she refuse a man whose invitation sounded like a song?

Dear Reader,

Favorite author Kasey Michaels starts off the month with another irresistible FABULOUS FATHER in *The Dad Next Door*. Quinn Patrick was enjoying a carefree bachelor life-style until Maddie Pemberton and her son, Dillon, moved next door. And suddenly Quinn was faced with the prospect of a ready-made family!

A BUNDLE OF JOY helps two people find love in *Temporarily Hers* by Susan Meier. Katherine Whitman would do anything to win custody of her nephew, Jason, even marry playboy Alex Cane—temporarily. But soon Katherine found herself wishing their marriage was more than a temporary arrangement....

Favorite author Anne Peters gives us the second installment in her miniseries FIRST COMES MARRIAGE. Joy Cooper needed a *Stand-in Husband* to save her reputation. Who better for the job than Paul Mallik, the stranger she had rescued from the sea? Of course, love was never supposed to enter the picture!

The spirit of the West lives on in Pat Montana's *Storybook Cowboy*. Jo McPherson didn't want to trust Trey Covington, the upstart cowboy who stirred her heart. If she wasn't careful, she might find herself in love with the handsome scoundrel!

This month, we're delighted to present our PREMIERE AUTHOR, Linda Lewis, debuting with a fun-filled, fast-paced love story, *Honeymoon Suite*. And rounding out the month, look for Dani Criss's exciting romance, *Family Ties*.

Happy Reading!

Anne Canadeo, Senior Editor

Please address questions and book requests to:
Silhouette Reader Service
U.S.: 3010 Walden Ave., P.O. Box 1325, Buffalo, NY 14269
Canadian: P.O. Box 609, Fort Erie, Ont. L2A 5X3

STORYBOOK COWBOY

Pat Montana

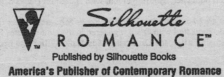

Silhouette
R O M A N C E™
Published by Silhouette Books
America's Publisher of Contemporary Romance

To my daughters, Julie, Pat, Marci *and* Jan.
Borne not under my heart, but in it.

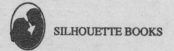 SILHOUETTE BOOKS

ISBN 0-373-19111-1

STORYBOOK COWBOY

Copyright © 1995 by Patricia A. McCandless

This edition published by arrangement with Harlequin Books S.A.

Printed in U.S.A.

Books by Pat Montana

Silhouette Romance

One Unbelievable Man #993
Babies Inc. #1076
Storybook Cowboy #1111

PAT MONTANA

grew up in Colorado, but now lives in the Midwest. So
far, she's been a wife, mother of four adopted daughters and a grandmother. She's also been a soda jerk,
secretary, teacher, counselor, artist—and an author.
She considers life an adventure and plans to live to be
at least one hundred because she has so many things to
do.

Some of the goals Pat has set for herself include being
a volunteer rocker for disadvantaged babies and teaching in the literacy program. She wants to learn to
weave and to throw pots on a wheel, not to mention
learn French, see a play at the Parthenon in Greece and
sing in a quartet. Above all, she wants to write more
romances.

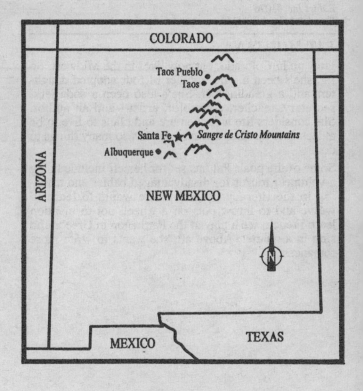

COLORADO

Taos Pueblo •
Taos •

Santa Fe ★ *Sangre de Cristo Mountains*
Albuquerque •

ARIZONA

NEW MEXICO

N

MEXICO   TEXAS

Chapter One

"Once upon a time... not so long ago, a tall, rugged cowboy rode his golden palomino, just like Rocinante over there, through the hills and across the wide arroyos outside Santa Fe. Like every good cattleman I've ever known, that cowboy was as tough as dried old cowhide and dern near as independent as a rattlesnake. And he went by the name of Chaps Marshall."

"What did he *look* like, Jo?"

Jo McPherson stopped forking fresh pine shavings into the horse's stall and brushed away tendrils of brown hair clinging to her damp forehead. Grinning, she waited for the young girl to spread the clean-smelling bedding across the floor. Adela reminded her of an eager young colt.

"Your turn today, Adela." Puffing a breath of air into her bangs, Jo led the sorrel mustang back into his stall. The horse nudged the young girl with his broad nose and plucked at her pockets for sugar. Watching, Jo realized how fond she'd let herself become of Adela, in spite of her resolutions of almost a year ago.

In fact, everything about the morning stable cleaning at Maravilla Ranch gave her a sense of satisfaction. Fresh feed and water, clean space, good grooming and exercise—those were all the horses required of her. She didn't even mind mucking out the stalls. Physical labor felt darn good these days and hardly made her sore anymore. Nothing that a good night's sleep couldn't repair. Most nights she could count on that now. The bad dreams almost never returned.

And ten-year-old Adela didn't have any problems. She was as tickled as a prairie dog in a bucket of peanuts as long as they made up new chapters to their ongoing cowboy story while she helped.

Jo latched the stall door and moved on to the next with Adela close behind. "So what *did* he look like?"

"Oh, Jo, he was *so* handsome. Like, really rugged."

Jo nodded. No brand-label, fat-money-clip city slickers for them. She and Adela had agreed that their fantasies had to be New Mexico-style, not Hollywood. "So *tell* me."

"He had sorta light brown hair," the fearless girl called as she led the big palomino into the spare stall. " 'Cept when he'd leave his hat off in the sun. Then some of it would turn kinda lighter."

She popped back into his stall to add fresh water while Jo shoveled out the soiled bedding.

"And he had green eyes. You know, green like the piñones."

A dark, earthy green. Jo nodded approval. "Nice touch."

"He was tall, but not *too* tall, and real...like...solid. Kinda square, and dusty...like an adobe— Oh!"

The girl's sharp intake brought Jo around in one swift motion. "What's the matter? Are you okay?"

"Look," Adela whispered. She grabbed Jo's arm.

"What?"

That's when she saw him. A cowboy, or rather the taut backside of one. A cowboy who was tall, but not *too* tall, done up in the blue chambray work shirt and body-hugging Levi's that Adela hadn't yet got around to describing. Wearing a dove-colored Stetson—Adela preferred gray over black—and boots that from this distance looked to be the color of the dusty beige earth outside the stables. He looked...like...solid. He looked...like... breathtaking.

The cowboy half turned. "Anybody here?"

All Jo could see beneath the shadow of his hat was a jaw that angled sharply, then veered to define a square chin. But it was enough to make her lean forward for a better look, enough to make her understand that *cowboy* was, beyond a doubt, the least appropriate handle in the world. This was no *boy* standing in the aisle of the Maravilla stables.

"Do you think he's real?" Adela whispered.

Jo took a deep breath and discovered she needed it. "Unless you know magic," she whispered back. "Have you been holding out on me?"

Adela's giggles brought the man completely around.

Cringing, Jo raised a finger to her lips. "Now you've done it. We'll have to come out, and after all the work we did conjuring him up, he'll probably just disappear."

Adela hung back, muffling laughter behind a small hand.

With a wink, Jo grabbed another fast breath and stepped out of the stall. "Can I help you?"

His hat still shadowed his eyes, but she could see the sharply defined geometry of his chin, the unswerving line of his wide mouth. His symmetrical nose squared at the end and lines bisected the flat planes of his cheeks around his mouth, not deeply—just enough to hint that if she could see his eyes, she'd probably find a smile there. A possibility that made her breathing grow shallow again.

"I'm looking for the trail guide." He hooked his thumbs into his jeans pockets and shifted his weight to one leg so that his broad shoulders mirrored the tilt of his hat.

Even if she couldn't see his eyes, she sensed this was a man who knew where he was going and had few concerns about getting there—in his own sweet cowpokin' time. Body language that triggered an automatic reaction, a wariness she'd brought with her when she'd left Denver at the end of the last school year. *Beware of a man who wields power.*

But she was being silly. Not every man tried to move the world the way Jason did. This was just another tourist—here today, gone by sundown. Besides, cowboys were *supposed* to be strong and self-reliant. The thought gave her a measure of relief.

"If it's Tuesday, you're looking *at* the trail guide." The words rang sharper than she'd intended, and she felt more than saw his reaction, a brief pause, possibly a frown. He took time to appraise her more closely.

"I'm looking for *Joe* McPherson."

He wasn't the first to presume the trail guide was a man. Usually she didn't let it bother her, but this time, she felt a twinge of disappointment. Yanking off her work gloves, she strode forward and stuck out her hand. "I'm Jo McPherson. What can I do for you, Mr...?"

"Covington."

Again he paused, his head cocking slightly, and she could imagine him squinting down at her, measuring her against his expectations of a trail guide. Disappointment shifted to annoyance when she caught herself raising her other hand to smooth her flyaway hair. Jamming her fist into a pocket, she watched him notch back his Stetson with a thumb, then reach out.

His grip was firm and engulfing, but that wasn't what caused her pulse to stumble. It was his eyes. They were the darkest green she'd ever seen, filled with the smile she realized she'd been waiting for, a quizzical smile that barely turned the corners of his mouth. A bone-melting smile.

"*Trey* Covington," he added, obviously unaware of her reaction. "I apologize for the typecasting, Ms. McPherson." He let her go but didn't move back even an inch.

Which did little to ease her panic. The warmth of his hand lingered on her skin. His nearness sent sudden awareness scurrying through her. In some corner of her mind, it came to her that his hand had been smooth and uncallused, too well kept. These were not the hands of a *gen-u-ine* cowboy. This man wasn't what he appeared to be.

That only served to increase her wariness. His face held too many of the qualities she and Adela fancied, such as eyes the color of the piñon needles and a shock of hair the sun had tipped light gold. She stepped away from the heat that seemed to radiate from him, that caused gooseflesh to skitter up her arms.

"Apology accepted, Mr. . . Covington." That cinched it. With a name like that, he couldn't be a cowboy. Or a fantasy. *Trey Covington* didn't wash, not next to names like *Latigo Stinson* and *Chaps Marshall* that she and Adela gave their cowmen. Trey Covington was a name that spelled money—with a Roman numeral III after his name.

Adela's giggle broke through Jo's ruminations.

"You can come out, Adela. Why don't you finish in the tack room? I'll be there to help in a minute."

Adela's face glowed with curiosity as she trotted by. She slowed near Trey Covington as if she were about to burst with questions. Jo marveled at her self-control, especially when the man touched the brim of his hat, his straight mouth softening into a full-blown smile that spurred Jo's pulse.

She almost wished Adela would bombard him with her questions, because he looked as if he meant to stay planted smack where he was until he got what he'd come for. And that could only mean trouble. Trey Covington stirred things she'd forgotten. He made her feel—

"Trail rides are posted on the far stable door," she blurted, interrupting the unwarranted direction of her thoughts. She pointed to the white cardboard schedule, then escaped into work, retrieving the pitchfork to heave a clump of shavings into the stall.

Trey just ignored her ignoring. Tugging his hat forward, he leaned a shoulder against the opposite wall as if he had all the time in the world. Out of the corner of her eye, she saw his smile settle into watchfulness.

"Tell me, Jo McPherson, Lady Trail Guide, what if today were Wednesday?" Only a glint of teasing warmed his gaze.

"Wednesdays the trail guide is Native American." She worked to maintain an air of brusqueness, flashing him a sideways glance as she pitched a last forkful of bedding into the stall. Dear God, she was flirting!

"I think I like your incarnation today better."

She would have sworn the angular planes of his face didn't change, yet his attention seemed to deepen, just ahead of the growing warmth in her cheeks. She'd thought she was beyond blushing. Trey Covington was awakening responses she hadn't felt in a long time.

"You should see the beard on Friday's version." She fought a grin, experiencing a rush she didn't want to think about. Much as she hated to admit it, she was hoping to see his smile again.

Trey looked amused, even congenial, but there was none of the tenderness in this smile that Adela's coltish departure had provoked.

And she was being a fool. Her imagination was putting in overtime. Real cowboys might be self-reliant, but only fantasy cowboys showed tenderness, and Trey Covington wasn't either kind.

Ducking into the stall, she spread the pine bedding and concentrated on reality. "How long did you want to ride?"

"I figure about three hours, out and back. I need to look at some acreage, and your boss tells me you know your way off the trails."

The change in his voice brought her back into the aisle. He was all business now—broad shoulders squared, eyes focused on a sheet of white paper.

"I have a map of sorts, but I'll need some help."

A man on a mission. Twice as unsettling. She resisted the impulse to sidle over and peek at the page. "I already have tour groups scheduled today."

"Your Wednesday scout is coming in for extra duty."

Taken separately, the lines of his face read serious, yet there was that sneaky smile again, creeping back into his eyes, goading an anticipation she didn't want to feel.

"You must have worked some kind of magic. Frank isn't usually so flexible with part-time help." She actually managed to hold his gaze, though another flush of heat crept to her cheeks. This was a man who could wield magic.

"Most people get real helpful when you cross their palms with silver."

Suddenly the air in the stable turned cold, as if a cloud had blown right inside and blocked out the sun. He'd said the words lightly, but their intent confirmed everything she'd sensed about him. Trey Covington was used to getting what he wanted . . . even if he had to buy it.

She should have paid attention to her first wariness. She should have remembered the only real heroes she'd ever known were those in stories. She knew this kind of man, knew what he could do to people. The dreams didn't let her forget.

Well, Mr. Rich Cowboy with the III after his name could ply his money and influence till his laughing green eyes crossed. All they'd buy him here were trail-guide services.

"Okay, Mr. Covington, when did you want to leave?"

"Mr. Covington is my father, Jo."

His tone darkened, but as quickly as she looked up, the tension pulsed away like a power surge, leaving no evidence of its passing—except that damnable smile. It was well-practiced—she could see that now—intended to oil the machinery of business, to get what he wanted. She'd known a smile like that before, too.

"If you'll call me Trey and point me at a horse, I'd like to leave right away."

This man was capable of far more than charm, and that stirred an inkling of fear. She avoided him as she led the palomino back into his clean space. Even the big horse wasn't immune to him, whinnying good-naturedly at this stranger when he was usually more inclined to snort and stamp.

"Rocinante?" Trey rubbed the brass plate on the palomino's stall door. "How could anyone name a beautiful horse like that Rocinante?"

"The owner thought it sounded romantic. He ended up having to sell him, so I guess he was an impossible dream."

She knew better now than to pursue impossible dreams. Five years of teaching had managed to wipe out most of her naiveté, and Jason had taken care of the rest—along with his son, Danny. She didn't believe in wishes coming true anymore, and the only dreams she knew were bad ones. She snapped the stable door bolt as if to lock away the memories forever.

"Don Quixote's nag," Trey murmured, fingering the latch she'd just closed. He slid it open and reached into the stall to rub the big horse's nose. "Perfect." Stepping inside, he began to saddle the horse. "I'll ride Rocinante."

Jo watched with an increasing sense of dread. Like Jason, Trey Covington wasn't a man who said, "If that's okay," or "Would it be all right?" He just decided what he wanted and went after it.

She should be glad all Trey wanted from her was her ability not to get lost without benefit of trail. Because once they finished his treasure hunt, she never wanted to see him again.

* * *

Cinnamon. Trey had smelled it the minute he'd stepped into the stables, could still smell it here in the morning air, over the dark brown scent of leather and horses. Sweet and spicy—exactly the way Jo McPherson had struck him.

"If you'll show me your map, I'll get an idea if your time estimate was right," Jo said gruffly, reaching across the space between their mounts.

Definitely cinnamon. She must have a piece of hard candy tucked away behind that smile, which wasn't so much shy as reluctant. Strange how she seemed to waver between spirited no-nonsense and cautious uncertainty. That fleeting wariness made her look almost . . . afraid. Jo McPherson added up to something perplexing. Intriguing.

And she struck him all right—right in the midsection—every time she called him Mr. Covington and turned those honey-colored eyes away from him. The banter between them kept changing. Disappearing. He didn't understand why.

He dug his father's meticulously annotated map from the pocket of his faded blue shirt and handed it to her, taking care not to touch her again. One brief handshake had been enough to make him aware of her effect on him. Heat.

Lifting his hat, he combed his fingers back through his hair, welcoming a cool waft of air. "That was copied from a survey done almost thirty years ago. I expect a lot of the landmarks have changed since then."

He watched her study the paper, reins slack as she sat on the saddle of the sturdy sorrel mustang she called Dusty. She was a tall woman, less than three inches shorter than his six feet, with the longest legs he'd ever seen graced by a pair of well-worn, body-hugging blue jeans. She was probably only a year or two younger than his twenty-nine years, as well.

Suddenly uncomfortable, he nudged Rocinante to put space between them. He hadn't appraised an attractive woman in a long time and now wasn't the time to start. One divorce and a year of casual dating should have been enough to teach him—a square peg with money didn't handle relationships very well.

"I think I know where this is." Jo's voice broke into his brooding. "Round here, landmarks don't change much."

She had abandoned even the qualified smiles, but that didn't stop him from watching her full pink lips, nor from feeling the heat. Damn it, he'd expected Jo McPherson to be a leathery-skinned old codger when the only thing about her that could be mistaken for a man was her name.

He'd have preferred an old coot. He didn't want a woman in his life right now, especially not a lady trail guide who was probably on the lookout for a wealthy husband. That was, no doubt, why she didn't like him much. His square corners never managed to conform to the wealthy Covington image.

At least that's what Cheryn had said. *You act like some rodeo-circuit rider instead of a respectable well-to-do banker.* After a year he could still hear her words. *Why can't you be like your father?*

He swiped a hand across the back of his neck and jerked his hat lower over his eyes. If he were smart, he'd keep his distance from Jo McPherson. Reining his horse back, he let her ride ahead toward the boundary of the property where he could see a cowhand working the fence line. At their approach, the man straightened and ambled over to the gate.

"Guacamole." He greeted her, touching the brim of a straw hat as white as snow against the coal black of his shoulder-length hair. "Be gone long?"

"Probably a couple of hours, Kody. We're headed up beyond Chimayo. Mr. Covington already cleared it with Frank."

The man's copper-colored face didn't alter, but Trey felt the rake of his dark gaze as he examined him. It occurred to Trey that *he'd* have reservations about sending Jo into the wilds with a lone stranger, too. Nonetheless, he must have passed inspection, because the man she called Kody unlatched the gate and swung it open without another word.

"If that was Wednesday's trail guide, he seemed a touch testy," Trey observed as Jo led them away from the trail.

"He's still training me for Sacagawea certification."

To his disappointment, the flash of mischief disappeared from her eyes as quickly as it had kindled. He should let it go. But the possibility that she might kid with him again was too appealing. "I thought he called you Guacamole." To his surprise, she stiffened.

"Just an in-house joke."

Giving the reins a twitch, she moved ahead, but not before he caught the color brightening her cheeks. Something about the nickname unsettled her, a reaction that made him want to know more. Only a burst of good sense held him back. He was here for one reason, and he couldn't let anything distract him—not even a pretty woman. A woman who should be called Cinnamon.

To the east, the Sangre de Cristo mountains stretched into the chaste blue sky, their slopes shadowed in bands of purple and crimson, just as he remembered. It was a good scene to take his mind off her, to bring back memories of his visits here with Grandpa Shel. Ever since he'd arrived yesterday, he'd been discovering familiar sights. Even the willows along the banks of the nearby washes seemed familiar... after twenty-some odd years.

His gaze returned to the woman ahead of him, and he felt again the pull of attraction. She was almost as slender as the willows, with the same windswept grace. He liked the way her dark hair lifted away from her face and brushed at her neck when she raised her straw hat.

There was something familiar about *her*, too—the way her eyes tilted slightly down at the corners, the flashes of distrust, the hint of sadness that didn't quite fade, even when she smiled. Sadness that reminded him of Billy.

The image of his serious five-year-old son, with knots of cowlicks swirling the front of his tawny hair, finally snapped Trey back to his purpose.

"So why are you looking for this land, Mr.... Trey? I didn't see an X marked on the map."

"I'm afraid Blackbeard never made it this far inland, at least not that I know of. The land belongs to my...client. He wants to get something out of it after all these years. Seems to think it can *make* him a treasure."

That was the only explanation he could come up with. His father's sudden notion was the kind of crazy scheme Grandpa Shel would have jumped at. But not his father, not the staid Vermont banker.

He needed to understand what was happening to his father since his mother died. He wanted this chance to do something to make his father proud.

The rest of his time was for Billy and his spring visitation, for closing the distance that had grown between them. In spite of the divorce, he was going to be more than just the proper father his own father had been. He intended to be a full-fledged dad.

"Your client could make a lot more money if his land were nearer Santa Fe. But I'm sure you're aware of that."

The edge in Jo's voice caught him off guard.

"Even this far out, though, land has gone up in value," she continued. "My landlady owns a parcel around here, and she says there are surveyors all over the place. People must want to buy, so your client can still make a bundle."

Again that unaccountable anger hovered in the air, and he didn't understand why. Didn't want it to be there.

She pulled her horse to a stop several yards from his. "Your client's land can't be too far from here." She seemed to be warning him to keep his distance.

Fine. He would follow her lead—stop getting caught in the evanescent changes of her hazel eyes. Turning, he pointed to a distant outcropping of salmon-colored towers. "My client mentioned rocks like those, like turrets on a castle."

His father hadn't mentioned them at all. His father had probably never seen them, but Trey recognized them. He'd been here before, he was sure, even remembered the scent of juniper spicing the bright air. It seemed Jo had led him unerringly to the land Grandpa Shel had bought years ago—the land right in the middle of the Covington family feud.

"Formations like those are pretty common, Trey. Let me see that map again." Taking the paper from him, she clicked her tongue, urging her horse through stubby brush, leaving low-lying dust hanging in the air.

Trey prodded Rocinante after her, concerned to know what had fueled more disapproval.

Fifty feet ahead, she jumped from the saddle. "According to your map, the property line runs parallel to those rocks. Look, it's been marked." She pointed to a bright orange flag staked close to the ground.

Some seventy-five feet beyond, another fluttering spot of orange caught his eye. Like a carefully laid line of desert flowers, flags stretched away from them into the brush.

"You knew about this, didn't you?" She squinted up at him. "Your client hired those surveyors, didn't he?"

"My client wanted an up-to-date measurement of his land, Jo. There's no law against that." The creases between her dark brows made him want to reach down and smooth them away.

"If I'm not mistaken, Mr. Covington, your surveyors were a little overzealous in their work. It looks to me like they've staked right into my landlady's property." She sounded irate—with a feisty indignation that suited her much better than sadness, that made the set of her mouth downright delectable.

"Hey, don't draw your guns yet, Cinnamon." He summoned a grin, raising his hands in surrender. "That's why I'm here—to make sure everything is handled smoothly."

"*Don't* call me Cinnamon!"

Well, he'd be damned if "smoothly" included trying to appease a spicy and much too appealing lady trail guide, even if what she said was right. Technically.

Technically his father could claim only half the land Grandpa Shel had given to his two sons. But his father always did a job thoroughly. Spared no expense. If Shelton Covington, Jr., paid surveyors, they would survey it all, whether his sister-in-law liked it or not.

"Wait a minute." Suddenly the meaning of Jo's words sank in. "You think they've marked your *landlady's* land?"

"I think I hear an echo."

"How can you be sure?"

"That I hear an echo?"

She was actually smiling now, letting him know she was glad she'd unsettled him. The effect was devastating.

He bit off an oath and swiped at the heat gathering at the back of his neck. Jo was too sharp to be pressed any further. She'd suspect right away if he showed more interest in her landlady.

But if her claim was true, her landlady was his father's sister-in-law. Her landlady was his aunt Meira.

That wasn't something he'd planned on, but suddenly it came to him that his father had. Shelton Covington, Jr., left little to chance. That was why he'd sent Trey to this particular trail guide. His father expected him to use Jo.

He should have known. He was probably crazy to think he and his father could find some kind of bond working together on this scheme. Even more crazy to think he could resolve the family feud. Both were impossible dreams. He'd definitely chosen the right horse.

"Well, Mr. Covington?" She glared up at him. "Just what do you mean by smoothly? I get the feeling that something strange is going on here. Does your client intend to sell his land, or what?"

"I hate it when you call me Mr. Covington, Cinnamon." Why was it he wanted to kiss her when what he should do was ride straight out of her life without looking back?

Instead he raised his hands and summoned all his sincerity. "Look, I'm not wearing a black hat. I'm not even armed. Smoothly means no bad feelings, nobody gets hurt, okay? My client just wants to do a little ranching." He tried for charming, but ended up somewhere nearer coaxing.

Neither of which had much effect on her, because she planted her feet solidly apart and glowered. "You mean, as in cattle ranching? He wants to raise cows out here?"

"Well, not exactly." He gave a shot at sheepish. To no avail.

"Then what—" she clapped her hand on her hips "—exactly?"

Trey grimaced and shoved back his hat. "I believe he's interested in camels."

Chapter Two

Settin' real tall in his black hand-tooled saddle, stone-faced Chaps Marshall scanned the scrub-dotted land and pictured it covered with cattle as far as the eye could see. Trouble was, that was too darned far. Gol durn animals would break through the fence and trample the widow Abigail's bean sprout patch. Durned if she'd let him take her niece Jenny to the ice-cream social then. Were the farmers and the cowmen ever goin' to be friends?

"Your client wants to raise *camels?*" Jo shaded her eyes with her hat as she squinted up at Trey, still mounted on Rocinante.

He nodded. "Large hairy beasts with long fuzzy eyelashes who don't need a lot of water. With the water shortage around here, they make more sense than cattle."

Though the lines in his cheeks deepened with the promise of a smile, she detected an undertone of seriousness. "This is a joke, right? Camels live in the Sahara and haul nomads and sheikhs around."

Sheikhs. The moment she said it, an adolescent fantasy wavered into memory—daydreams of being carried away on a camel, of a slender boy with dark eyes and strange gold coins in his pockets.

But she hadn't been a teenager when Jason's dark magnetism, and the veiled manipulation of his wealth, had played right into that fantasy. He'd taught her not to trust in sheikhs, not to believe in magic-carpet rides.

"You're in New Mexico here, Mr. Covington, not the land of Aladdin." She was as angry at herself as she was at him, and she clung to the clear-cut emotion, wishing he'd fight back instead of watching her so intently. So distractingly.

"Damn it, Jo, will you stop calling me Mr. Covington?"

Humor softened his demand, as if names had already become a game between them. She'd be smart to move directly into a real temper, especially in the face of his lurking smile. Trey was too easy to like, too easy to trust, and she was losing ground by more than inches.

"I won't call you at all as soon as I get you back to the ranch and out of the sun...which you've obviously had way too much of already. Whatever you need to do out here, you'd better get to doing it, because I'm heading back—" she glared at her watch "—in exactly ten minutes." She swung up onto the mustang's back, aware of his watching her, aware of little else. She fought to keep from looking at him, to hold on to protective self-righteousness.

"What I need is to ride this survey line, and I suspect it will take more than ten minutes. You wouldn't abandon a cash customer now, would you, Cinnamon?"

He was still teasing, his mouth tilted temptingly at the corners, but she saw subtle changes, too—a set jaw and an air of certainty that translated into rock-solid determination. A look she'd seen too many times in the past. By God, if he offered to cross her palm with silver, she'd gallop off into the sunset.

But the only thing he offered was that lingering amusement tinged with that damnable self-assurance. And sunset was a good eight hours away.

"Wouldn't I?" She glared at him, hoping he would believe she deserted riders regularly...and without conscience. But she didn't, and she knew she wouldn't this time. Frank would fire her faster than a bull could dump a rodeo rider. Besides, she needed the job. Besides...

She had to see this through. Another hour, and Trey Covington would mosey out of her life with whatever it was he'd come for, leaving her more determined than ever to stay away from men with money and power.

Reluctantly she directed her horse after his, following from one fluttering flag to the next, bright orange banners that did little to cheer her failing mood. The markers doglegged to the east, flapping between patches of creosote bushes and clumps of paddle-shaped cacti. In the distance, high mountains brushed the cerulean sky with blue-green tips of pine and fir. With a jolt, she realized she'd hardly turned her attention from Trey since they'd left the stables.

Usually she sought the arid beauty of the countryside for comfort. The wide cloud-scudded skies and undemanding solitude gave a measure of peace to her still-grieving heart.

Land like this shouldn't be owned by people interested only in profits.

"It snows here in the winter, you know." She watched him guide Rocinante into a wide dry wash. Even at a distance, she couldn't shake her heightened awareness of him.

"It frosts on the Sahara," he hollered back, studying the ground.

"There are rattlesnakes and coyotes and all kinds of prickly things. There may even be cougar in the mountains."

That brought his head around, but not from alarm, because his grin had returned, deepening the creases beside his mouth and filling his eyes with that droll amusement. "There used to be camels here, too." He nudged his horse forward, holding her gaze.

He was baiting her with well-practiced charm, and she was doing a terrible job of resisting. "I don't believe you." She shot the words back feebly.

"Government project," he affirmed. Touching his heels to the palomino's sides, he guided the horse toward her. "Didn't work out, though. Civil War kind of interfered. But the camels did fine. Toward the end of the century, they had to catch them to get rid of them."

His horse fell in beside hers, so near that his leg brushed against hers. She felt his heat as if they shared a closet instead of miles of open range. "So...so why would anyone want to bring in more?" she managed to ask.

At first he didn't answer, only considered her more closely.

"They thrived here once," he offered, still watching her. "Guess my client figures they can do it again. Domestic camels are raised on feed, so they don't overgraze the land. I understand that's a problem around here."

It was clear he'd done his homework. He was answering objections before she could gather her wits enough to think them up. Outwitting her, when all she wanted was the satisfaction of roping him and dropping him in his tracks.

"One of those morning TV talk shows did a special on an alpaca ranch around these parts. I really think that's what put my client onto the plan."

"I know about that ranch, Trey. They folded a year or so ago...just pulled up stakes and moved away." That should put her ahead, should give his rope a good solid yank.

"They *sold* out, Jo. Demand outdid their supply. I understand they made a bundle of money."

Money. She could almost hear the twang of a jerked lariat followed by a sharp snap, leaving her with the dangling end of a failed rebuttal and a knot somewhere in the vicinity of her heart. Trey had a way of making her forget this was all about money. But she wasn't ready to give up.

She nudged her horse to keep up with the pace he was setting. "Those were alpaca, Trey. People buy their long silky wool. But who'd pay for a mangy old camel?"

"A mangy white female can sell for a tidy hundred thousand dollars."

All she could manage was a soft gasp. That only served to light a twinkle in his eye—and stoke her frustration.

"But the plain old brown ones are what most people want, usually to rent. Others want stud service for breeding. The biggest markets, though, are zoos and circuses. And parades."

"For children," she murmured in amazement. She could picture Trey leading one of those hairy beasts with colorful tassels dangling from its ears, could visualize a couple of giggling children on top. Could see his smile.

Whoa. Her imagination had just kicked in again, reading fun and virtue into dollars-and-cents business information. Trey wasn't interested in entertaining children. He was here to make a profit.

"Why doesn't your client sell the land? Buy some cheap desert property and make camel money somewhere else?"

"I don't see why you object to camels, Jo." Trey swept an arm toward the horizon. "What with people around here communing with spirits in the air and hearing strange humming sounds in the earth, seems to me camels should fit right in."

He almost appeared to be trying to persuade her... when he had no reason to. That only added to her worries.

"I don't care if he wants to raise walruses. It's not the plan I object to, it's the attitude. Your client hasn't even moved in, and already he's a pushy neighbor." She spurred her horse to get away from the way his eyes kept weakening her defenses.

"I admit he overstepped his boundaries, Jo, but I can assure you his camels won't break down the fences and get into your landlady's crops."

She swung back to face him. "How did you—?" His joking tone made her bite back the words. *Did* he know about Meira's plan to lease her land for organic farming? He seemed to know more than she'd even thought to suspect. How could she still be so naive and unquestioning?

"I don't know anything. But let me guess." He caught up with her. "She's going to plant corn, right? High as an elephant's eye."

"This isn't Oklahoma and this isn't a joke."

She might have attributed the lopsided shift in his mouth to charm, but it came to her that there was irony in his smile—and more than a touch of regret.

The worry she'd been grasping like a lifeline suddenly wrapped tightly around her heart. Trey knew more, a whole lot more than he was letting on. He was holding something back, and it related to Meira.

That was the way of powerful men; charming a woman at the same time they took over, manipulating a situation to suit them. She knew.

And Trey had taken over, as naturally as an alpha wolf. Looking around, she realized they'd already covered part of the return trip to the ranch—with him in the lead.

"You're a fast learner," she muttered. "Not many newcomers get their bearings so quickly."

For once, he turned away to scan the countryside. "I spend a lot of time outdoors—backpacking, camping. You learn to watch for landmarks."

She knew immediately that he'd left more unsaid. It was almost as if... he knew this country.

"Trey, have you—"

"If my client's going to carry out his plans, there's a possibility he'll want more land. Do you think your landlady might be willing to sell?"

"*What?*" Her saddle creaked as she whirled to confront him. "Is that what this is all about? Is that why my landlady's land was surveyed?" Suddenly it became crystal clear. "That could well constitute trespassing, you know. Haven't you heard of boundaries?"

"Like the ones you're guarding so carefully?" His quiet words hung in the warming midday air, punctuated by the dull rhythm of the horses' hooves on the hardpacked earth.

"I . . ." She'd been ready for almost anything but the heat that flickered in his eyes.

Who was this man? How could he read her so accurately? Keep her roller coastering between distrust and. . . She didn't want to give a name to the panic in her heart. She couldn't let him continue that line of questioning.

"If you're interested in my landlady's property, I suggest you talk to her yourself." She made no attempt to soften her tone, only clutched the reins to keep her hands from shaking.

"That's what I'd planned to do, Jo. Before I learned she has a protector like you."

"I'm *not* her protector. I'm her tenant."

"I thought maybe you were her friend."

Foreboding shot through her. Trey's simple observation threatened all the more because it was true. She'd been young Danny Harcourt's friend, too. The memory made her want to spur her horse and ride away as fast as she could.

But Meira wasn't a child. *She* wasn't a child. "Meira is perfectly capable of taking care of herself."

"With a big Eastern banking tycoon?" He waggled his eyebrows Groucho-style, and the tension that had been building between them eased.

She slipped her arms out of her jean jacket and tied the sleeves around her waist, glad for an excuse to look away, to avoid the teasing that had returned to his eyes.

"My landlady already made arrangements to farm that land, so you don't have to waste your client's time by even asking. I'm sure she's not interested in selling."

Not now. But if Jo didn't help her, Meira might lose her Seeds for Tomorrow project. What Trey couldn't capture with that quixotic charm, she was sure he would pay for, and she had no reason to think Meira would be any more immune than she was to either brand of persuasion. Meira might be easily hornswoggled by a wealthy camel rancher. Trey's client probably didn't give a damn about other people's dreams.

Trey slowed Rocinante. He needed to back off still further, take more time with Jo.

He could tell by the gentling of the land and the clusters of cottonwoods that they weren't far from the ranch. Once they arrived, he'd have to put her out of his mind. He wasn't about to use her to accomplish his father's purposes.

"Okay, Cinnamon, if your landlady won't sell, I just hope moving camels in next door won't lead to a range war."

Jo urged her mount ahead, and he couldn't read her reaction. Damned if he didn't seem compelled to try to make her smile, in spite of her obvious dislike for him.

"It strikes me as more than a little suspicious," she called back, "that just when my landlady decides to profit from her land, an obstacle suddenly shows up."

He gave Rocinante his head to catch up with her. "I've been called a lot of things, but never an obstacle." That won him a sideways glance and a trace of a rise in her brow.

He had to stop this teasing because he wasn't interested in a woman who couldn't accept him for who he was, rough edges and all.

"My being here now is just coincidence, Jo. My client's wife died a year ago, and I think he's looking for something a little different to...take his mind off things."

Her gaze wavered, and for an instant he caught sight of another kind of loss before she looked away. What was it she was hiding behind those defenses?

"Look, I'm here to solve problems, not create them. I give you my word I won't be party to anything that would hurt your landlady." No matter how much he wanted to help his father, he wouldn't do anything to harm Aunt Meira. Suddenly it was important that Jo believe that.

At last she turned distrustful eyes to him. "Why would you promise *me* anything?"

"Because I'm not in the business of hurting people." Especially not a lovely woman who already concealed too much sadness. "Do I have to remind you that villains do *not* wear white hats?"

"Yours is gray," she retorted. Pulling her horse to a stop, she swung down from the saddle.

In a flash, he was on the ground following her, headed for the gate he'd failed to notice—because he'd been so intent on her.

She beat him there, but not to the latch. His hand closed over hers, and her skin felt soft and warm. Suddenly he was aware of everything about her—the satin glow of perspiration across her cheeks, the tendrils of damp brown hair clinging to her slender neck, the dark, confused honey of her eyes before she spun away. She left behind the spicy scent of cinnamon...and heat that shafted through him.

"I'll get the horses," she called, tugging her hat down to cast her face in shadow.

Trey swung the gate wide to let them pass, then closed it quickly and caught up before she could remount. Falling in step beside her, he took the reins and continued to walk. They were covering the distance to the stables too quickly.

"Tell me about your landlady, Cinnamon." He heard her short huff of protest at the nickname, but he couldn't trust himself to look at her. Not until this heat subsided.

"Sizing up the opposition, Mr. Covington?"

Their thrust and parry of names made him grin. Deliberately he paced himself slower, hoping to extend his time with her, watching her dusty black boots outdistance his gray ones.

"I prefer to call her a neighbor. Tell you what, let's trade information. I'll go first."

Her steps slowed momentarily, then stretched out again. "I'll listen, but I won't make any promises."

"No promises expected." And she couldn't have chosen a better time to remind him. He'd had his share of promises, and they hadn't been worth the wedding certificate they'd been printed on. He wasn't in the market for any more.

"My client," he began, denying the heat still lingering in his limbs, "is president of a family banking firm. Silver spoon, social register, country club membership on his birth certificate and all that. Patron saint is Miss Manners."

She rewarded him with a side glance that failed to hide her interest, and he realized he was still trying to make her smile. He was still too aware of her nearness.

"I doubt he's seen this property in New Mexico more than once. Land that can't be golfed on or built on usually isn't land he's interested in."

"So he's fat and bald and wears sharkskin suits. Does he smoke cigars?" she challenged.

Impudent. The tantalizing glimpse made him grin. She had no idea how appealing her saucy humor was. "Actually he's tall and lean, and he has a full head of white hair. My mother... always said he was the most handsome man in town."

Damn, he hoped Jo wouldn't put his hesitation together with his reference to his mother and come up with client-equals-father. She was too sharp a lady for him to be so careless.

"And he's a cousin of J. R. Ewing," she concluded.

He gave a short whistle. "Not that big a tycoon. He's a hard-nosed businessman, but he's not ruthless." And *he* was enjoying Jo entirely too much.

"What's his name?"

He shifted the reins to his other hand to buy a little time. That was one question he hadn't anticipated. "Shelton. Junior," he added. Jo would consider omission of the Covington surname dishonest, he was sure. One little deception shouldn't bother him so much.

"Okay, your turn. Tell me about your landlady." He kept his distance, afraid she might read his sins in his face. Out of the corner of his eye, he saw her shake her head solemnly.

"She couldn't be more different from your client if she tried. She's an artist... your basic blithe spirit. The only use she'd have for a silver spoon would be to mix paints... or to serve up cat food. She takes in every stray that gets word of her within a four-state area."

She'd relaxed, almost seemed to be enjoying herself in this task of proving to him his client didn't stand a chance. "You sound pretty fond of her." Distress flickered across her face, the reaction caught him by surprise.

She sidestepped away. "That's not your concern."

Aw, hell. He had no good reason to try to cheer her, no excuse for getting himself in a lather over a female trail guide with an attitude. "So what does she look like?" he muttered.

She seemed to consider whether or not to even answer. "She's round," she finally replied, "like a dumpling. And she colors her hair. And your riding time is up, Mr. Covington."

He looked up to see her stride away, leading the little mustang toward the stable door.

"Ho, wait a minute there, Cinnamon. What color?"

Her eyes flashed at the nickname. "Orange," she pronounced, continuing her retreat to the stable.

She was exaggerating, he was sure, had probably made up every bit of the information about his aunt. But he didn't care. Her feistiness was worth it.

"Women don't color their hair orange," he proclaimed, following her, with Rocinante close behind.

Jo stopped long enough to shrug. Dark brows rose over eyes that sparked. "Suit yourself. She *does* color canvases, though, with wonderful paintings of spirits. The ones that live in the atmosphere around here." She circled her finger in the air like a whirligig. "But she prefers New Age music to the Taos hum."

For the first time all morning, she really smiled, with a satisfaction that brightened her changeable eyes and filled them with challenge. "Not exactly a matched set, are they?"

She was telling him she considered his mission foolish at best. More likely, impossible. A smile like that made a man do foolish things. Like follow her into the stables when he should hightail it in the opposite direction. Like want more time with her when he should be forgetting the things she made him feel. Like think about kissing her lips.

From the stall where she unsaddled Dusty, Jo watched Trey follow her into the stables. She waited impatiently while he attached crossties to Rocinante's halter and pulled off his saddle. When he tossed his Stetson onto a peg and reached for a rub rag, she realized he was going to stay. That was when she made the mistake of stepping back into the aisle.

"One of the hands will take care of the grooming, Trey." She wanted him to leave. She wanted Trey Covington out of her life. More immediately, she wanted him out of the close confines of the stable aisle before his easy charm and laughing eyes broke through her defenses any further.

Ignoring her, he began to rub the animal down. "Will you talk to her, Jo?"

She'd known he would ask, just as surely as she knew she should refuse. She had no reason to get involved in Meira's decisions, and the morning had shown her she hadn't yet learned how to deal with Trey's kind of persuasion very well.

With every smooth stroke of his hand across the horse's dusty coat, she felt her guard slip another notch. Awareness rippled across her skin just as it had when he'd brushed her hand at the gate.

"What do you want me to say?" She crossed her arms over her denim shirt as if to ward off his effect. The threat of a wealthy Eastern banker had to be taken seriously. She knew the danger of a powerful man.

Trey stopped rubbing the animal and straightened to look at her, undermining her resolve even further. Heat seemed to shimmer between them in spite of the coolness of the stable.

"Say whatever you think, Jo. Tell her about the land survey, about me, about my…client's plan. Give her your opinions. I want her to have time to think about it all before I talk with her." Without waiting for her reaction, he moved to the other side of the horse.

She let out a slow breath, glad that he'd moved away. He was too assured, too confident. Too appealing.

Between the horse's hooves, she watched his dust-laden gray boots shift and sidestep as he worked his way back from the horse's neck, rubbing and reassuring with sounds that came to her as calming murmurs more than words. Sounds that affected her like a song—soothing her defenses bit by bit. The man was hypnotizing, and she was losing her ability to resist.

Snatching up a body brush and curry comb, she joined in the grooming, busying her shaky hands, diverting her errant thoughts. She kept the big animal between them.

"You want me to tell her my opinions? That seems rather reckless of you, considering your client's interests are at stake here." She managed to sound businesslike in spite of the frog that had taken up residence in her throat.

"No bad feelings, nobody gets hurt, remember? Even in New Mexico, the farmer and the rancher should be friends."

She could feel him trying to charm her again. "Just long enough for the rancher to persuade the farmer to sell." She shot back the words in self-defense.

"You are a hard woman, Miss Jo," he drawled softly. "How can you say such a thing to a poor honest cowboy? Now tell me, have I been anything but trustworthy and true the whole time you've known me?"

Teasing warmed his voice, and she could picture the smile that went with it, could feel its warmth draw her. The horse's flank twitched in complaint as she increased the vigorous brushing.

"The whole time I've known you has been all of three hours, Hopalong. I hardly consider that a true sample. Besides, *camel herder* would be more accurate, and I have serious doubts about poor. *And* honest."

Trey didn't answer. Silence filled the air that had hummed with activity and banter only seconds before.

"Trey?" Darn it, after all her barbs, had she finally succeeded in insulting him? *"Trey?"*

For the first time since she'd started to work here, suddenly the stable felt . . . lonely.

Chapter Three

Chaps strode down the boardwalk, stewin' 'cause folks in Santa Feliz still considered him a stranger. Spurs janglin', his dusty boots drummed the boardwalk till he stopped to talk to Miss Jenny at the Dry Goods Store. Asked her if she'd speak to the widow Abigail about buyin' her land. Later, Jed told Jenny the stranger looked jest like that thar outlaw Jody Whales. But Jenny wondered how a fine-lookin' man like Chaps could be an outlaw. And how a new-comer could know the widow Abigail's name.

Jo cut a wide swath around the horse's rump and almost fell over Trey where he kneeled to examine the animal's leg. Hands fumbling on his shoulders, she struggled to right herself and felt his hands close around her arms. He rose slowly, holding her gaze, stretching to his full height just inches from her. She could feel his heat. And her own.

"Reckon I'd prefer to be called ranch hand," he murmured.

He stood so close she could see flecks of jade in his laughing eyes. His fingers tightened ever so slightly, wresting a shallow gasp from her that brought the compelling scent of a man who'd spent the morning outdoors. The temperature in the stable rose by degrees. Her heart all but stopped.

"Or maybe Sheikh," he said, his voice rough like corduroy. His hands began the slow ascent up her arms. "Do you think I could wear a turban, Cinnamon?"

She stared into his darkening eyes, searching for an answer, trying to ignore the trembling that had begun inside, that followed the movement of his hands. "I think...you'd look...like you just washed your hair." She managed to croak out the words.

His gaze flickered with humor, then slipped to her mouth, snatching away the last of her breath. Making her heart beat like a tom-tom. Leaving her unable to move.

All she could think was that she'd lied, because in a turban, Trey would *not* look like the boy next door. He'd be mystery and danger—mesmerizing eyes peering from exotic fabric that covered sun-gilt hair and hid a half-smiling mouth. The mouth she fought to keep from looking at now.

In a turban, he wouldn't be able to kiss her.

"I think...you should get a turban," she said weakly, stepping back to stop herself from leaning into his kiss. She slipped from his grasp as something inside her flared with wanting at the clear intentions written in his eyes.

"And I also think," she said, taking another shaky step, "that I have a tour group in half an hour. One of the workers will finish grooming Rocinante.'' With the brush still in her hand, she backed away, watching Trey swipe fingers through his hair. She was relieved beyond belief that he didn't pursue her.

"You'll talk to Meira, Jo?'' he called across the distance growing between them.

"I'll talk to her,'' she answered, intent on getting away, "but only for her benefit. So she'll be prepared for you and your client.''

"That's enough.''

It was more than enough. It was the last thing she'd do for Trey Covington, because she would never see him again.

Trudging across the visitors' parking lot, she struggled with the erratic beating of her heart, with the too-vivid memory of their close encounter. She fought to regain a proper sense of outrage. Jason had never disturbed her this completely.

Slowly she became aware of an engine roaring to life and the rising volume of a country-western song. A black Jeep rolled into view, its shiny paint gleaming through a film of dust, the sides open where doors should have been. As it drew nearer, she recognized Trey, saw him touch the brim of his dove gray Stetson. Another rush surged through her. Close on its heels came the dread.

He didn't smile, just wheeled by, leaving behind a yellow cloud and a clear impression of a firmly set jaw. And a new-car sticker in the back window.

A new Jeep. She jerked her hat down and dug a cinnamon drop from her jeans. The implications were all too clear—ready money and an extended stay. Meira was in real trouble.

She had no choice now but to warn Meira. She had to remember everything that had happened this morning so she could prepare Meira for Trey's skillful—and over-powering—persuasion.

Trey had said, "Talk to Meira," but she'd do more than that. She'd prepare Meira for every subtle little—

On the third step of the ranch house porch, Jo stopped dead in her tracks.

Trey had called her landlady by name.

A loud screech announced her arrival as Jo braked the little blue minivan at the curb. Jumping out, she dashed up the sandstone walk, barely noticing the bright red geraniums blooming in ceramic pots at the front of the adobe house. Her heart still thrummed—because she was in a hurry, she told herself. Because she hated playing scouting party to Trey's wheeling and dealing.

At the front door, she pulled off her white hat and clutched it to her chest, closed her eyes and tipped her head back, drawing in the lavender scent of lilacs that lined the path to her apartment in the rear.

Eyes still scrunched shut, she reassured herself one more time: Meira was an independent woman in her fifties, a woman who did not need help to run her life. And Trey Covington was just a businessman doing a job, a man good at remembering names, that was all. She *had* mentioned Meira's name during their parley, she was sure.

And her other reactions? Her eyes snapped open and she straightened with resolution. Any woman with hormones would be attracted to Trey Covington. But *this* woman knew what a man with money and influence could do.

Shoving her hat back onto her head, she hammered on the wooden screen door. "Meira? Are you home?"

"I'm coming, just a minute." The bright voice carried over the faint strains of Windham Hill, and a sprightly figure, almost a head shorter than Jo, appeared in the doorway. "Jo! I'm so glad you're here."

Clamping the stem of a paintbrush between her teeth, Meira wiped her hands on her blue smock, then opened the screen door. It gave a wiry whine. "Come in, come in!"

Jo stepped into the cool interior and ignored a twinge of guilt. She'd stretched her description of Meira a little. Well, more than a little. She could have said Meira was ... full-figured, but that hadn't seemed appropriate with a stranger. Trey *was* a stranger, she assured herself, no matter how quickly he'd maneuvered himself into her life. A rich stranger, out to get Meira's land.

Following Meira inside, she watched her pat the corkscrew tendrils of hair creeping from the edges of a purple paisley bandanna tied around her head. Hair that wasn't exactly orange, she acknowledged with another twinge. More nearly a soft shade of the color of Meira's favorite tabby cat, Flannigan.

"Come have some iced tea, Jo. I need a break, and you always have such interesting things to tell."

Jo sighed. "I'm afraid not today." If only her exaggerations had sent Trey galloping back to New York, or wherever it was his client tycooned. But she knew no story was crazy enough to discourage a man like Trey.

Settling into the rocker near the window, she waited for Meira to pour golden tea into glasses on the table near an easel. Flannigan jumped up and curled into her lap.

"Now, tell me everything, Jo. It's all over your face, and it's a strange mixture of good news and bad." Meira handed her a filled glass.

"I'm not sure any of it's good. A man hired me at the stables this morning to help find some land."

"That sounds interesting." Meira scooped two heaping teaspoons of sugar into her tea. The spoon jingling in the glass sounded like music from a carousel.

"I'm afraid it's not that simple." Jo hesitated, remembering the man who'd weakened her defenses, who'd made her forget to breathe. "I'm pretty sure the land he was looking for is adjacent to yours."

Meira's stirring slowed. "And the bad part?"

"His client hired those surveyors you told me about. They surveyed his property...and yours." And Trey had stepped across *her* boundaries.

Meira's light blue eyes squinted into a frown. Her spoon circled slowly, automatic and forgotten. "What was his name?"

"Trey. Trey Covington."

The spoon stopped.

Jo's heart lurched. She was almost certain Meira recognized the name.

The slow stirring resumed. "Did he say what his *client's* name was?"

Watching Meira closely, Jo sensed the same thing she'd felt with Trey, that Meira knew more than she was revealing. Something strange *was* going on here. Something she shouldn't be getting involved in.

"His client's name is Shelton."

Meira's face paled.

Jo felt her stomach tighten. Whatever Trey's client was up to meant no good, and Meira recognized it immediately. "Meira, what's wrong?"

"Wrong? Oh, Jo, nothing, nothing at all." Meira seemed to pull herself from somewhere far away to offer a faint smile.

To her surprise, Jo could find no fear in her eyes, only uncertainty.

"Tell me about this Trey Covington." Meira's brows rose. "Aha. I see we've come to the good part."

"Wrong." Jo set the rocker into motion, busying her restless fingers by scratching behind Flannigan's ears. "He dressed like a cowboy, but his style was more like a snake-oil salesman."

Meira actually laughed. "Was he handsome? Was he nice?"

Jo hoped the warmth creeping up her neck wasn't as obvious as the color returning to Meira's cheeks. "He was…thirty-something. About six-foot, light brown hair, square chin. Most women would say he was handsome. I guess some women would call him nice," she ventured, remembering everything nice about Trey—his deep green eyes, his half smile. His teasing humor. She remembered everything disturbing, as well, like his standing so near she could have kissed him. Like her wanting to kiss him.

"I see," Meira answered.

Jo suspected she *did* see, far more than she wanted her to, far more than she wanted to admit to herself. All the way home, she'd tried to believe Trey wasn't one of the bad guys.

"Does he know you're telling me this?" The misgivings were all but gone from Meira's eyes.

Jo nodded. "He asked me to talk to you. His client may want to buy your land."

"Buy my land?" Just as quickly as she'd brightened, Meira's face fell. "Oh."

The barely audible word faded away, taking Jo's brief hopes with it.

"Did he give you any details?" Meira asked quietly.

"Yes. His client is looking for something to do since his wife died."

Meira's head came up.

"He wants to put in a ranch. He wants to raise *camels*."

"Camels?" Meira's eyes filled with moisture before she looked away.

Jo rose abruptly, sending Flannigan leaping away with an offended meow. She stalked over to the pitcher, a sense of foreboding washing over her as she added to the glass she'd hardly drunk from.

"He said his client is a big Eastern banking tycoon. Wants to recover something from his land after owning it for so long. Seems to think camels will make him a fortune, though I can't see how renting them to zoos and circuses could amount to much." She hurried on, avoiding Meira's questioning gaze.

"Trey said you might need help dealing with him. I told him I didn't think you'd want to sell. I told him you could very well take care of yourself," she added hopefully.

With that, Meira pulled a tissue from a pocket, dabbed her eyes, blew her nose. Mumbled something that sounded curiously like, "Presumptuous young pup."

"Of course I can take care of myself," she said with what sounded like indignation. Retrieving a paintbrush from her other pocket, she aimed the tip at Jo. "I want you to go right back to this Trey person and tell him if his client has a . . . proposal, he'll have to present it to me himself."

"But Meira—"

"Anybody named Covington would stay at La Fonda. You march right over there and tell him I don't need any help."

"Meira, if you don't need—"

"Find out more about this...this client of his, Jo. Better yet, bring him here to talk to me. Sending a woman to do his job," she muttered. "What's the matter with these young people?"

"Meira?" She had planned never to see Trey again.

"Well, go on. Let's get things moving."

Meira might as well have taken a broom and swept her right out the door. The screen slammed behind her, adding a *clap, clap, clap* for Meira's performance, because that's what it had been, Jo was sure—bravado in the face of serious distress. She'd never seen Meira act so... strange.

Behind her she heard the screen door whine open again. "Jo," Meira called, "be sure you find out if he's married."

"Find out if he's married," Jo grumbled for the bazillionth time. She strode along the shaded street toward the Plaza, warmed by the five-block march in spite of the cool morning air.

She didn't want to do this. Especially since Meira's request—*command* seemed more accurate—smacked of matchmaking. Still, that gave her some reassurance, since it was a whole lot more like Meira than her pale face and the tears that had shone in her eyes yesterday afternoon.

Meira's reactions continued to haunt her, even more so since she'd called La Fonda. Meira had been right—Trey was staying there. And Jo was about two bricks short of a pueblo to get involved in whatever this was all about.

Her stomach growled, and she stepped up her pace. She'd see Trey once more to deliver Meira's messages. To remind herself that *all* wounds heal, eventually. Her reaction to him yesterday simply meant she was coming back to life. Then she'd treat herself to *huevos rancheros* with Christmas chili and go on to the day-care center. *Adiós,* Trey Covington.

Digging a cinnamon drop from her denim blazer, she crossed into the Plaza. The sidewalk under the portal of the Governors' Palace was already filling with Native Americans spreading blankets to display their wonderful creations of silver and turquoise jewelry. She forced herself not to use them as an excuse to stall, made her feet carry her across San Francisco Street and mount the steps to the modest entrance of the pueblo-style hotel. Reluctantly she pushed open the door.

The atmosphere inside La Fonda was always inviting, with its massive wooden vigas spanning the ceiling, its earthen red floor tiles and dark leather and wood furniture that absorbed the hubbub of people in the lobby. But this was one morning she didn't want to be here.

Drawing a deep breath, she stepped up to the young man behind the inlaid-wood front desk. "Would you ring the room of Trey Covington, please? Tell him Jo McPherson is here to see him." Coming so early and unexpected should give her the advantage.

"I could, but I'm afraid you're too late."

"He checked out?" News like that should have brought relief, but it only reduced her to uncertainty. And a whisper of disappointment.

"Hey, he's over there in the patio restaurant. Probably holding a place for you." He winked.

Trey had obviously made an impression on the young man, but was *her* conflict so obvious? With a man like Trey, a woman shouldn't wear her emotions like a big sombrero. *This* woman shouldn't even be having emotions. She was here to represent Meira's interests—and beat a fast retreat.

Apprehension dogged her steps across the lobby. If she had any sense at all, she'd leave right now. Remembering Meira, she continued to the entrance and peered cautiously into the restaurant.

Into an oasis—that was the first thought that came to her mind. A tall ficus tree rose among tables dotted with aqua napkins, and overhead a ceiling of skylights lit bright murals on the walls and filled the room with morning sun.

How fitting that a man dealing in camels would choose such a place to stay. The Sheikh of Santa Fe. Another time she might have laughed, but this oasis held hidden dangers.

She didn't need psychic powers to know that Trey could bring danger to her life, and change. He already had, and she wasn't ready. She'd never be ready for a man like Jason again.

A shiver rippled across her shoulders. She shouldn't have come here to see Trey.

"Jo. Jo McPherson."

Trey saw her hesitate and knew she'd heard him over the restaurant buzz. Pushing up from his table, he strode toward her, bent on reaching her before she turned and was gone.

He hadn't meant to see her again. It was bad enough that every attempt to put her out of his mind had met with total failure. Now he'd have to start over from square one.

The air seemed to warm by degrees as he drew near her, and instead of the scent of expensive perfume, he caught again a whiff of cinnamon. Sweet and spicy.

"Jo, are you alone? Have coffee with me."

"I'll only stay long enough to deliver a message."

She let him guide her through the tables, staying just ahead of his touch, and he sensed that given the slightest provocation, she'd spook and run.

"We need to talk, Trey."

He'd expected her to be angry about yesterday's charade, but she seemed almost nervous! He held her chair and watched in surprise as she settled on the edge. Her cheeks carried a hint of the rose color of her blouse, almost as if she were blushing, and her hair fell in rich brown waves to her shoulders and escaped across her forehead in self-willed wisps. She looked fresh and scrubbed. Wholesome. The effect was beguiling. When she looked up, he understood again how those wary eyes could be a man's undoing.

He waited until the waiter finished filling their cups.

"No trail guiding today?"

She focused on the coffee. "Wednesday is Kody Sanville's day. The man who opened the gate?" She didn't smile, and he could almost feel her distrust.

He considered her over the top of his mug, knowing he should cut to business, take the upbraiding he was due for deceiving her about his aunt, and hear Meira's message. Then send her on her way.

But her uneasiness added to her appeal, made him want to see her smile again, in spite of his resolve to stop that folly. In spite of his intentions to put her out of his mind.

"Look, Trey, I talked to—"

"So what are you doing today?"

She set her cup down. "I thought you wanted a go-between."

"I do, but there's no reason why we can't be . . . good neighbors, is there?"

"There are a lot of reasons. Beginning and ending with my messages. I have to leave, so if you want to know what she—"

"Okay, Cinnamon. Tell me about Meira."

He had her attention now. Something in her attitude had changed—she sat straighter, watched him more closely. There was an uncanny perceptiveness about her that warned him that somehow he'd stepped onto dangerous ground.

"You talked to her, right? What was her reaction? Was she willing to listen?"

"She listened."

She paused for a swallow of coffee, and he felt as if she'd taken control of the conversation. He suspected he was about to experience her ire after all, and he braced for her charges.

"She asked a few questions." She waited another beat. "I wouldn't say her reaction was exactly positive."

He watched her with growing concern. Had she convinced Meira he was a scheming rogue and a grasping land baron? Had she taken up Meira's cause and persuaded her to disown him as a nephew? "I didn't expect her to be exactly thrilled. What did she say?"

"She said she could take care of herself. That you'd sent a woman to do your job. I believe the term she used was 'presumptuous young pup.'"

He didn't even try to hold back a whoop of relieved laughter. "Uh-oh, looks like I goofed already. Not likely she'll talk to me now. What do you think?" Aunt Meira hadn't changed one iota. Thank God for that.

The shock on her face left no doubt that she hadn't expected his reaction.

"I think you'd better stop laughing and start looking for someone else's acreage. She said if your client wants to buy her land, he'll have to ask her himself."

"But Jo, that's great!" He hardly realized he'd reached across the table until he felt her hand tense beneath his, saw the sparks in her eyes. She looked vulnerable and defensive, but there was more—the same look he'd seen at the stables.

She didn't move, but he felt her tremble, felt his own reaction to her. One touch of her soft hand and his body tightened. One look at her face, and he knew she felt it too, the heat, the attraction. It smoldered in her eyes like dark gold smoke.

Then she pulled her hand away, clasped it with the other around her coffee mug and held on as if for dear life. When she glowered across at him, he realized he'd misread her, remembered that ice could make smoke, too. What he'd seen in her eyes rose not from desire but from the anger he'd been expecting all along.

"Now it's my turn to ask questions." She said each word precisely, the gleam in her eye predicting problems he hadn't even dreamed of.

"Trey, how do you know my landlady's name?"

Chapter Four

Chaps followed Miss Jenny around the Dry Goods Store. Said he jest wanted to check on supplies in case he'd be needin' to set up camp somewhere. The widow Abigail, she told Jenny she wasn't interested in sellin' her land, so Jenny wondered why Chaps might be thinkin' of staying. But wonderin' wasn't anything compared to what she thought when the little boy came in, shoved his hat back jest like Chaps, and asked for him to buy him a licorice drop.

Trey choked on a mouthful of hot coffee that seared all the way to his toes. "How do I know your landlady's name?" Good Lord, hadn't Meira *told* her he was her nephew?

Obviously she hadn't. Which raised an unforeseen, and critical, question. Why the hell *not?*

"You said her name yesterday, Jo, I'm sure. When we were trading information." She had, hadn't she? He didn't want to out-and-out lie to her. "I told you about Shelton, and you told me about Meira, don't you remember? It's such an unusual name. A name you don't forget."

He had visions of scrambling left and right, evading a bulldogger who wouldn't be satisfied until she'd yanked his feet right out from under him and watched him land . . . hard.

"No, I don't remember, Trey. You acted as if you knew her." Jo looked ready to pounce with a hot branding iron, and if she picked up on his failure to say *Mr.* Shelton, he would really get burned.

Damn, he'd never been good at deception. This time wasn't proving any different. "Wouldn't she have said something?"

"She acted as if she knew *you.*"

"But she didn't *say* so."

"No, but—"

"Well, there you are." He reached for the coffee carafe, avoiding her searching eyes, expelling a slow breath to cool his reaction to the lasting imprint of her hand. He had to get her to drop this until he found out the reason for Meira's silence.

At the same time, part of his mind was already working on what Meira could possibly be up to. Maybe she was trying to keep the feud between her and his father. From what he could remember, that would be like her.

"I owe you for acting as go-between, Jo. Her message is more than I'd hoped for." He risked a glance into those too-predictable eyes and wasn't surprised to find suspicion still lurking there. When she stopped him from refilling her mug, he knew she'd come to a decision.

"I have to leave."

Immediately he wanted to change her mind. "Wait a minute. I thought today was your day off."

She huffed her impatience. "Some of us don't keep the leisurely schedules of the rich and acquisitive. I'm due at a day-care center, so if you'll excuse me..."

"Daycare? What happened to the lady trail boss?"

"If it's Wednesday, I'm on rug-rat patrol. Full-time jobs are hard to come by in Santa Fe."

It hadn't occurred to him that Santa Fe would offer anything so practical as daycare. He thought of the sleepyheaded little boy upstairs with the baby-sitter. The little boy who didn't cry anymore. Didn't laugh much, either.

"I'll bet you're a good teacher. The kid at the stables sure admired you." He was stalling, he knew, fishing for more information...about the day-care center. He didn't need to know more about Jo.

She stared into her coffee mug, her eyes darkening as they had yesterday.

"Did I say something wrong?" He hadn't meant to call up her fleeting shadows.

"I *was* a teacher, but I left education. Daycare is different." She pushed back her chair. "I have to leave."

"Wait. I'll walk with you to your car. Hold on while I get the bill." He couldn't let her go yet.

"I'm not driving."

"Then the least I can do is take you to work." He searched the room for the waiter. "Tell me how daycare is different," he asked, to keep her from getting up, to steer away from whatever haunted her. For a long moment, he thought she wouldn't answer.

"I taught middle school," she said, studying the mug again, her thumb scrubbing the rim. "Twelve-, thirteen-, fourteen-year-olds. They're neither fish nor fowl at that age." She hesitated. "Lots of . . . problems surface."

"And a lot of rampant hormones." He tried for a lighter tone, to coax her from whatever memories she was battling. "Anyone who'd teach kids that age has to be invincible. Or crazy. Which are you, Jo?"

That brought her head up. If anything, the shadows seemed to have deepened. "Obviously crazy, or I'd be out of here by now." She set the coffee mug away.

"I thought you had to be a certified saint to teach daycare," he said hurriedly. "To handle all those diapers and . . . purple dinosaurs." He was gratified to see a faint hint of amusement.

"Fully certifiable is probably more accurate." Her uneven smile was edged in irony.

How would Jo deal with a kid like Billy? "Little kids have problems, too, don't they? What about kids of divorce?"

She considered him more closely. Unexpectedly her gaze dipped to his left hand where he curled it around his own coffee mug, to the finger that no longer wore a gold band.

"Over a year ago," he answered, surprised that the admission no longer bothered him. What did bother him was the little boy upstairs who didn't come for hugs anymore. Who wouldn't sit on his lap.

"You're right, Trey, little kids hurt, too, but they don't take drugs. They don't tote guns. They don't run away."

She pushed back and stood, and he knew he'd stirred hidden ghosts again. Hastily he threw down several bills and grabbed the napkin-wrapped chocolate doughnut.

Maybe little kids didn't run away, but they withdrew; they held everything in until all you could see was the sadness in their eyes. Just like Jo McPherson.

He followed her out of the restaurant, catching up with her as they entered the lobby. "What time do you have to be at work?"

She checked her watch and frowned. "Ten minutes ago."

"There's a phone over there. Give them a call while I run up to my room. I'll have the Jeep brought 'round and meet you on the sidewalk." Before she could turn him down, he touched a finger to her chin and watched her face mirror his own surprise. "Don't say no. I'm the one who made you late."

Lengthening his stride across the lobby, he wondered if she'd even be there when he came back. He should have known better than to touch her again. It only stirred more shadows in her eyes, made him want to know more about her. Made him want to smooth away the hurt.

If she fled, he wouldn't be able to find her. "Jo!" He spun around . . . and caught her heading for the door. "What's the name of the day-care center?"

She stopped abruptly, and guilt flickered across her face. "De Vargas."

Her unexpected answer made him grin. He reached to tip his hat but remembered he'd left it upstairs with Billy. Unwilling to wait for an elevator, he headed for the stairs. The less time he took, the less time she'd have to reconsider flight.

He didn't want her to leave. Because of Billy. Daycare would give his son a place to be with kids while he finished his father's business.

That was the only reason for his anticipation.

He'd caught her running away and startled the name of the day-care center right out of her. Jo watched Trey extend long legs down the corridor and gave up the idea of running out again. Resolutely she put away the image of wide shoulders, pearl-buttoned shirt, tight jeans. Even without his Stetson, Trey looked like a freshly shaved version of the make-believe cowboys she and Adela created. Except that their cowboys didn't have hands that had never worked a posthole digger. Their cowboys didn't throw down ten-dollar bills to cover the cost of a couple of cups of coffee.

Their cowboys weren't divorced.

Meira might want to know Trey's marital status, but nothing about him was of any consequence to *her*. She'd wait, but only because if she walked now, she'd be more than half an hour late to work. Late because of him, so he owed her a ride. After that, he wouldn't be around to remind her of Jason or young Danny ever again. They were memories that belonged in the far reaches of her mind.

Picking up the phone, she dialed the day-care center. The line was busy. With a sigh of impatience, she tried again. It rang eight times before someone answered.

"Jo! Can you hold a minute?"

The director's voice faded, and in the background, Jo could hear children shouting and babies crying—a minor state of pandemonium, at best. Of all mornings to be late. Bonnie needed her there. Why was it that attractive, wealthy divorced men always seemed to interfere with her job?

At last Bonnie returned, and Jo assured her she'd be there in minutes. Hanging up, she hurried to the door, wondering if she'd find Trey's Jeep. Parking spaces were rarely available, and double-parking on the narrow streets around the hotel was next to impossible.

Outside, she glanced both ways, searching for the jaunty black Jeep. She spotted it halfway up the block, angled into the curb. For a moment, the flow of tourists on the sidewalk thinned, and she caught sight of a tall figure with sun-tipped hair and a striped cowboy shirt. She started toward him, sure that it was Trey, recognizing the way he hung his thumbs in his pockets and cocked his shoulders at a tilt.

Strange that a little boy from the crowd would approach him. Maybe the child was lost. Her steps slowed as she watched the boy turn beside Trey, hang his thumbs in his jeans pockets and rest his weight on one leg, throwing his body into a slant.

The stance matched Trey's exactly.

She stopped. Looked more closely.

The boy's head just topped Trey's belt, but he seemed long and lean in his striped shirt and narrow jeans that stretched all the way down to his dusty little boots. A shock of hair lopped onto his forehead—a lot like Trey's did, hair that was a lighter shade of brown and tipped gold by the sun.

The child was a miniature of Trey.

Trey glanced down at the boy, and she saw his straight mouth soften into a smile, the same smile he'd shown Adela at the stables yesterday. But more caring.

Trey had a son.

She whirled and started away.

"Jo! Over here."

For a moment, she slowed, her heart hammering as if she'd seen a ghost. The likeness between Trey and the child was undeniable. She couldn't ignore the frightening sense of her life playing itself over again—same song, second verse—another wealthy divorced man with a son. Images of Jason and Danny Harcourt flooded her, threatening her with tears.

"Jo."

A firm hand caught her arm and brought her to a stop. She felt as if she were in the middle of a game of statues and someone had just shouted, "Freeze!" Except that Trey hadn't shouted. If he had, she'd have kicked into a run, left him and his pocket-size heir forever in her past. But his tone was quiet, edged with authority.

"Come on, Jo. I'm about to get a ticket."

She couldn't find her voice to protest as he steered her through the tourists. As they neared the Jeep, she saw no sign of a small child, only a policeman tapping his pencil on a pad impatiently.

Dear God, she must have been hallucinating, her worst dreams come back to haunt her in broad daylight like a mirage. That's what she got for slumming with a camel merchant, a man with dark eyes and green bills in his pockets.

"Climb in, Jo. We are *out* of here, officer." Trey handed her into the passenger side and saluted the policeman. Throwing himself into the driver's seat, he started the engine and whipped the vehicle into traffic, flicking down the volume of a Garth Brooks song.

"That was close."

A boyish grin wiped away whatever chagrin she thought she'd detected in his face.

"Seat belts, everybody."

"Aw, Dad."

This time she really did freeze. Her heart stopped altogether, then took up its painful hammering again. Despite of what felt like paralysis, she couldn't keep from peering into the back seat.

The little boy sat in the middle with Trey's big gray Stetson resting just above his eyebrows. He was struggling with his seat belt. Each time he leaned forward to try to snap it, the hat flopped over his eyes.

"Jo, meet my son, Billy. Billy, say hello to Miss Mc-Pherson."

All Jo could see was the bobbing top of the Stetson, and beneath, solid little arms and busy fingers intent on mastering the uncooperative snap.

"Billy?" Trey's voice took on a parental edge.

A click, and the small fingers stilled. One hand rose to push the hat back slowly, revealing wide-set eyes above a thumb tip of a nose and a broad, serious mouth edged with chocolate.

Light green eyes. Like the early spring growth of the piñones. Distrustful eyes.

Though she stopped the gesture, Jo couldn't stop the wish. She wanted to reach out and pat him. She'd seen that look before.

"Hello, Billy. You can call me Jo. You did a good job with that seat belt."

His head dipped to check his accomplishment, tilting the hat off-balance and back over his face. Once again, the small hand shoved it back, and serious green eyes considered her from the shadow of the low-riding brim.

Jo let her amusement show only in her raised brows. His head dipped again, but not before she saw the slightest trace of answering humor in his eyes. The same humor she'd seen in his father.

"Billy?" Trey repeated.

Jo winced.

"Hello." Billy all but whispered.

"Hello, what?" Trey pressed.

"Hello, Miss Muck Fishin'."

Oh, dear. Jo felt tears and laughter start from the same well. Trey's attempts at being a father were painfully familiar, but Billy's efforts to respond were precious.

"Trey, I really prefer Jo to...something more formal." She couldn't repress the grin that told him Billy had won this round.

"How 'bout *Miss* Jo?" He half smiled, looked almost sheepish. "Billy?"

Lord, he didn't let up. "Trey, that's not—"

"Is your name really Joey?" Billy interrupted, curiosity overcoming his distrust.

"Yes." She answered before Trey could intervene. "Yes, it is, but it's the girl kind, so it's just Jo, and I'd really like you to call me that, okay?"

"Okay." He picked at a scab on his arm, then glanced up anxiously at Trey. "Jo."

"Okay, Jo," Trey echoed. "Better tell me when to turn."

"Left at the next corner. Down two blocks on the right."

She rode the rest of the way in silence, barely aware of the music coming from the radio, holding tightly to the urge to turn around and coax the little boy to talk. He sat so silent she couldn't tell if he watched out the windows or if he traveled in a private world inside himself.

Trey didn't talk, either, but she refused to ask him why he hadn't mentioned his son. The song on the radio warned her to do her dreaming with her eyes wide open, reminding her she shouldn't waste breath challenging Trey at all. His money, his persuasion, his son...none of them had anything to do with her. Her eyes were wide open, and she was about to say goodbye to Trey and his son forever.

"Over there. You can let me out in front. Thanks for the ride." She reached for the door latch and waited for him to come to a stop. "Goodbye, Billy. I hope you have fun in Santa Fe."

"Hold on, Jo. We'd like to come in and look around. Billy's been stuck with me or a sitter all week. He could use a little time with some kids."

"You want . . . ?" Jo felt a sense of forewarning at the same time she sympathized with the little boy. But she wouldn't let herself get involved. "Trey, summer enrollment is full. They're not accepting any more kids."

"That's okay. We can still take a tour, can't we?" He pulled the Jeep into a space in front of the building.

"I'll have to ask the director. She may be too tied up." Possibly literally. She hurried up the wide walk to the double doors. "I'll make sure things are under control. Wait for me in the front entry."

She sped inside, away from Trey and the little boy who threatened to steal her heart with his big unhappy eyes. She couldn't let this happen again, couldn't make the same mistake she'd made with Danny Harcourt.

Outside Bonnie's room, she stopped and slipped off her jacket. Summoning a composed face, she pulled open the door. A buzz of activity greeted her.

"Talk about timing." Bonnie sat in a circle of youngsters on the floor. "All the crises have passed, so now you show up." She looked cheerfully indignant.

Everything appeared no more disorderly than usual, and the children all seemed occupied. A few looked up from the floor, waiting for Bonnie to continue reading.

"We sent Kelly home with a temperature and mediated two fights," Bonnie continued. "Since then, things have settled into our regular state of chaos. So what's your excuse?" Her gaze strayed to the doorway. Widened.

"Did we find the right room for the five-year-olds?"

Trey's voice brought Jo around in one motion. He stood just inside the room, with Billy in front of him.

Billy no longer wore the Stetson, and his hair looked as if one of them had wielded a comb, a futile effort thwarted by a knot of cowlicks that split a thatch of hair into curls on his forehead. The chocolate was gone from his mouth.

"Uh-*huh*." Bonnie turned back to Jo, her smile growing.

Jo might have managed to wish Trey away, but she could no more have ignored Billy than she could have made him eat worms. Her heart went out to the little boy despite of all her resistance. He looked twice as unhappy about the situation as she was.

"Bonnie, this is Mr. Covington. Bonnie Carlson, the program director. And this is Billy, who must be five years old. Am I right, Billy?"

Chin bumping his chest, he nodded. Jo could see him scanning the room out of the tops of his eyes.

"Billy, would you like to come draw with Matt and Jessica?" she asked.

He moved a step closer to Trey, his head still down.

"Go ahead, Billy. Show them how you draw Captain Magic." Trey took his hand and walked him into the room.

"Captain Transformer," Billy corrected softly, but he followed Trey to the table and examined the children's drawings from behind Trey's elbow. Head still lowered, he reached for a marker, slid his little bottom onto a yellow plastic chair and accepted the paper Jo handed him.

"Why don't you show Mr. Covington around," Bonnie suggested.

"After all I've left you exposed to this morning, I wouldn't think—"

"Oh, go on, Jo. Everyone will stay under control awhile longer. Probably," she added, still grinning.

"Thanks, Bonnie." Trey gave her a nod of appreciation.

There was that well-practiced charm again, and that bone-melting smile. Jo recognized the softening in Bonnie's eyes and remembered the way women had reacted to Jason. Only time and distance had let her understand that everything Jason had done had been for his own purposes.

She'd been so naive and unsuspecting. But she wasn't that way anymore.

"Okay, Trey. I'll give you ten minutes."

Trey followed Jo into the corridor and watched her stride away as if she were anxious to get this over with.

He should be, too. All he needed was to assure himself this was a good place for Billy. Then he could get on with his father's business. Once that was accomplished, he could spend all his time with his son.

Jo moved down the corridor, keeping up a steady stream of commentary about the center. As quickly as he came up beside her to look into a room, she was gone, leaving him with only the faint scent of cinnamon—and a sense of something missing.

What had changed? She was like a firefly, flitting away as if she were afraid of him. She made him want to catch her, to find out what caused those fleeting lights and darks.

"This is Teddy Bear Corner." She waved him to the doorway of an empty room where toys were strewn across the floor. "The toddlers are outside right now." Without looking at him, she was off again.

Damn it, he shouldn't miss the attraction that had played between them, shouldn't want to slow her. The gentleness he'd seen in her eyes for Billy was gone, too.

He caught up with her before she reached the next room. "Look, if you're mad because I'm keeping you from your job, just show me what relates to Billy."

"Since there aren't any openings, it doesn't really matter what I show you, does it, Trey? But you'll get the full tour, because we always treat our visitors graciously. A good part of our budget is contributions."

So *that* was what this was all about. Money. She must still regard him as a threat to Aunt Meira. And Meira sure hadn't given her any reason to think otherwise.

Jo was still questioning his motives, his honesty, just as she had at the stables. What could he do to convince her he was as trustworthy and true as a cowboy?

At the next door, she stopped. "Once the toddlers are out of diapers, they come to the Little Kids' Room." Stepping in, she moved to the side so he could follow.

A cluster of squealing children lay sprawled across the floor all mixed up with a litter of rabbits. Smack in the middle sat a little blond girl trying to cradle a squirming lop-eared black ball of fuzz.

Lord, the little girl reminded him of his sister Becca when she was little. "You would have had to drag my sister out of this room. She'd want to kidnap a rabbit—or one of the kids—and take them home."

Jo looked as if she were surprised his life could include anything as ordinary as a sister. She slipped by him, but this time she waited a moment before moving on.

Maybe talking about family made him seem less threatening.

"These are some of the older kids." She led him to the next doorway. "We take them up to age eight during school breaks."

Though she didn't invite him, he stuck his head in and considered the possibilities. "Those blocks would have kept my brother Ted busy all summer. He likes square corners and neat stacks. And Mitch would have been as happy as a moth in a blanket factory with all those books."

He could feel her watching him as they leaned around opposite sides of the door; he could sense her wavering defenses. He was on the right track.

"Now Andy, he would have needed to be moving. He was the hyperactive one. Loved to dance. Still does."

"Another brother?"

"Yep, the last."

She let him fall into step beside her as they approached the end of the corridor. Outside the last room, she leaned against the doorframe. Tilting her head, she reconsidered him.

"Where would you have fit in all this, Trey?"

There was no sarcasm in her tone. She really wanted to know. But an honest answer would probably send her flying to the nearest emergency exit, because he knew without a doubt he wouldn't have fit in here at all. Places like this had only round holes.

"I don't know. I'm not sure I was cut out for all this."

Curiosity widened her eyes, and for a moment he thought she'd ask more. Instead she entered the room.

"At the risk of stating the obvious, this is the nursery." Walking to the nearest crib, she scooped up a small figure in a marshmallow of a diaper and a short white shirt that rode up above its round belly. Cradling the baby in her arms, she rocked and crooned and tickled its cheek until its face crinkled into a smile.

No question where Jo belonged.

Disappointment caught him unprepared when she lay the baby back into the crib and stepped out the door.

''Okay, that's the tour, Trey, and Billy's had time to play with some kids. Now I have to—''

''Wait. Where do they go for recess?'' He wasn't ready to leave her yet, wasn't ready to say goodbye to this woman who vacillated between gentle care and prickly determination for reasons he didn't understand.

''Come on, Jo. Let's give Billy a little more time. Show me what's outside these doors.''

Which would she be this time, the lady or the tiger? Before she could object, he pushed open the double doors and stepped out into bright sunlight.

Chapter Five

Miss Jenny watched Chaps hoist another bundle of supplies to his broad shoulder, then held the door of the Dry Goods Store while he carried everything out to his wagon. An honest-to-goodness Conestoga wagon, he told her, smilin' that real slow grin. Why didn't she come on out to see...maybe go for a ride? Sure enough, that wagon was a sight to behold—just like Chaps. But nothin' on God's green earth would git her up on that seat beside him.

Shouts and laughter mingled with the metallic squeak of swings in flight. Small feet crunched through pea gravel, and a breeze rustled the leaves of tall cottonwood trees. It seemed to Trey that little kids clamored everywhere, scurrying up bright red ladders, crawling through blue tubes, wiggling down yellow chutes like a swarm of diapered monkeys working hard at having fun.

"Billy would love this!" He saw Jo relax into unconscious affection as she intercepted a chubby little guy wearing a diaper that was slowly descending toward his knees.

"These have to be the toddlers. I've never seen a better toddle in my life."

She nodded, failing to hide amusement that let him relax, too. Kneeling, she hitched the diaper up. "There you go, Jimmy." A smile finally took shape as she sent him back to his chase.

"Do they let visitors play, too?" Trey ambled along beside her, keeping an eye on the bundles of energy that raced around them while he enjoyed watching Jo. The children absorbed her so much she'd forgotten to avoid him.

"Of course Billy can play. . . if the class comes outside before you leave."

"Actually I wasn't asking for him." He lobbed an imaginary basketball toward the hoop at the end of a paved area at the side. "I taught my sister how to play." He gave her the full breadth of a grin, determined to win her over. He thought he saw her relent another notch.

"Miss Jo?"

A little girl with round dark eyes and braids planted herself in front of them. Her dark features reminded him of the man at the ranch, the man Jo called Kody.

"Fix my stwaps. Pweeze."

Jo knelt to take up the slack in her overall straps, and the girl cupped her hands to whisper into her ear.

He could tell the girl knew Jo. Trusted her, just like the little boy, Jimmy. She was a natural with the kids—full of play and encouragement and nurturing. It wasn't difficult to imagine her being just as giving with the awkward teenagers she'd taught, with boys who fought all the conflicts—and expectations—of growing up. The image made him want to win her trust all the more.

The little girl pulled away, and he saw Jo shake her head, exaggerating a frown that sent the child into giggles.

"Do, *too,*" she declared, her dark eyes dancing.

"Do *not.*" Jo rose, still glaring. "Now git!" She gave one braid a tug.

The girl dashed away, singsonging, "Miss Jo got a boyfwend."

Jo bent to brush the knees of her jeans. "This is all there is to see, Trey, so if you're ready...?"

She wouldn't even look at him, which was just as well, because up until now he hadn't thought to wonder if she had a "boyfwend." All of a sudden, he did wonder, and the question bothered him. Her reaction bothered him even more.

And he still wasn't ready to leave her.

"What about...?" Wandering away, he surveyed the rest of the playground. "By God, what about *that?*"

It was a wagon—an old Conestoga wagon from the looks of it—resting against one of the big trees in the far corner. A wagon with a bright green cover!

"What a great idea." He crossed the distance quickly, heard Jo's boots scuff through the gravel behind him like a dawdling kid. At least she was following.

Running his hand over the wagon's smoothly sanded surfaces, he marveled at the bright yellow paint and the electric blue wheels. "When I was a kid, I wanted to drive one of these. Never managed to find one in Vermont, though. Especially not a redecorated one like this."

"You're from *Vermont?*"

He'd caught her curiosity again, which gave him another chance to talk about his family, to call back that flicker of trust.

But suddenly she was on the move. Dashing by him, she pounded up the wooden steps at the back of the wagon while, from inside the green cover, a whimper headed rapidly toward a howl.

"Charlie, you know you're not supposed to be in here alone."

Jo's gentle scolding made him wish he were inside the Kermit-colored cover with her instead of some little kid.

Slowly the crying quieted. A little boy with glasses like two big O's stuck his head out the front with Jo right behind. He glanced at Trey, then turned, still snuffling, and wiggled up onto the fire engine red seat.

Jo waited until he was safely settled, then stepped nimbly over the seat. "Okay, Charlie, you're going to drive those mules right to the sheriff's office." She handed imaginary reins to the boy.

Charlie swiped the back of his hand under his nose and took the pretend reins.

"Atta boy." She slipped a hand around his waist and started bouncing. "What a bumpy ride!"

Charlie bounced, too, and Trey heard his delighted giggle. He obviously trusted Jo completely. Also, Charlie was sitting exactly where *he* wanted to be.

"Say thar," he hollered. "I'm the sheriff of this here town. Stop them mules right now, mister." He pointed a finger gun up at them. "Hand him over, Miss Jo."

"Uh-oh, Charlie, I think you're caught. Better give me a hug before you go to jail."

All smiles, Charlie slipped eager hands around Jo's neck, then turned and leaned toward Trey. He caught the child under the arms and lowered him slowly to the ground. The moment was unexpectedly poignant.

It had been too long since he'd played with *his* little boy, too long since he'd breathed the sweet scent of a happy overheated child. Too long since he'd felt unquestioning trust.

Jo waved. "Go on back to the swings, now, Charlie."

Trey knew he'd have to move quickly. Testing the sturdiness of the wagon's front wheel, he grasped the side and swung up.

"*This* is where *I* fit in, Miss Jo." Headed west, away from Eastern living, free of bankers' hours and the onus of dollar signs. "Take a ride with me, Cinnamon?"

He'd thought sharing the wagon bench would be no different from riding with her in the Jeep—an opportunity to talk without the chance for her to run away as she'd damn well done ever since they'd gotten here.

But he'd been wrong.

Too late he saw the magnitude of his miscalculation. The seat was barely wide enough for them to sit shoulder to shoulder, and the air up here seemed incredibly warm. Suddenly he was too much aware of her, too conscious of the heat that seemed to erupt between them— and the alarm in her eyes. Too mindful of the ride he'd started them on.

But he couldn't stop now. Stomping his boots onto the footboard, he snapped imaginary reins. "Gee! Haw! Giddap, you stubborn mules."

Her arm grazed his as she straightened and again as she unbuttoned the cuffs of her rosy shirt and rolled the sleeves to her elbows. Even through his shirt, her touch felt like a brand. She must have felt the heat between them, too . . . or else she was fixing for a fight.

"I hope your mules aren't dumb enough to follow your orders, Mr. Covington. You just sent them on a zigzag path."

So it was to be a fight. He was glad to see her feistiness return, would much rather see her striking sparks than flying off like a fretful firefly.

"Don't know much about driving mules, Cinnamon. At Billy's age, I was dreaming about riding horses and being a cowboy. Guess I never outgrew that dream."

"Silly me, I thought you *were* a cowboy."

Her breath skimmed his cheek, and he inhaled the faint scent of cinnamon, sweet and spicy...with a bit of a bite. Unexpectedly he knew just how sweet her lips would taste.

"Trustworthy and true, wasn't that what you said, Trey? The hat and boots sure had me fooled."

This time he didn't stop himself from turning, from catching her chin between his fingers. "And I thought you were a schoolmarm, Miss Jo. A mighty sassy one, if you ask me." He saw the flare in her eyes just before his mouth closed over hers.

She tasted of candy...and more. She tasted of woman, warm and moist. She tasted of Jo, her lips full and firm beneath his. He wanted more, more of *this* woman.

He felt her stiffen in tandem with the tightening of his body, then slowly yield as he opened his hand to cup her jaw, to deepen the kiss. Her lips softened, moved beneath his. Then stopped.

She pulled away, not looking at him. He could see her shoulders rise and fall unsteadily.

So did his.

What could he have been thinking? "Look, Jo. I'm sorry. That shouldn't have happened. I never mix business with—I mean, I'm here for business. As soon as I can get my...client together with Meira, this whole thing will be finished and you can stop worrying. I promise my client will make a good offer. She'll make a tidy sum on the deal.''

This time what he saw in her eyes was more than sparks.

"You think you can ride in here on your rent-a-horse with money and charm and just walk away with people's dreams in your pocket. Well, let me tell you, Mr. Trey Vermont-Cowboy, I intend to help Meira hold on to her dream. Your client doesn't *have* enough money to buy that land, and you don't have enough charm to talk her out of it.

"Now, get out of my way." She stood, nearly losing her balance. He reached to help steady her, but she pulled back, eyes ablaze.

Which just made him want to kiss her again.

"Trey, if you don't get down, I'll—I'll scream, I swear I will.''

With what was probably his last vestige of good sense, he vaulted over the side of the wagon, then turned back to help her down. But she'd already disappeared inside the green cover, her boots beating an angry staccato. She stomped down the stairs at the far end and set off in long strides.

He should go after her. He should try to make peace. Whether she stormed away or decided to stand in the middle of Meira's land with fists planted on her hips, she was a threat. She could keep him from fulfilling his father's request. She could perpetuate the family feud.

Damn it, he didn't need the frustration of trying to please another woman with a hang-up about money. Using Jo to get to Meira might work for his father, but he wasn't doing a very—

He stopped. Uttered an oath. Checked to see what little ears might have heard. But the area was deserted.

Surrounded by empty playground equipment, he recalled his mother's advice, repeated so often the year before she died. "Remember, you're a Covington," she'd urged, as if the words alone could somehow make him bridge the distance between him and his father.

As much as he'd loved his mother, it was advice he hadn't been able to follow. He'd never be like his father.

But he was acting like him now. Damn. Clenching his fists, he stalked across the playground, sending gravel flying.

It didn't matter whether Jo installed her stubborn, appealing self in the middle of that land or not. He didn't need her help. He'd convince Aunt Meira in his own way, not his father's.

But first he needed to spend time with his son.

Storming through the back door of the day-care center, he ate up the length of the hall, searching for the room where he'd left Billy.

The director intercepted. "Billy's waiting for you in the front office, Mr. Covington. And Jo McPherson asked me to give you a message. I hope it makes sense." She smiled dubiously. "She said to assure you she'll do all she can to fight the camels."

Jo finished a page of the romance novel and discovered she didn't remember one word. Meira's old rocker squeaked faster as she started back at the top of the page.

"He cupped her cheek with his callused hand and—"

She slammed the book closed. "Darn you, Trey Covington!"

Flannigan raised his furry head and considered her stoically from his napping place amid jars of paint-brushes on a nearby cart.

"He had no right to kiss me, Flannigan." She slapped the book on the windowsill and stood, sending several more cats darting away in search of less disruptive surroundings. She wished the feelings Trey had ignited were so easily shooed away.

"He had no right to just disappear. Without a *word*."

Flannigan regarded her through half-closed lids, then laid his head back down, the tip of his tail twitching.

"You're no help at all. I wish Kody would get here."

She shoved up the sleeve of her baggy green sweater to check the time. Meira had said he'd be here at four-thirty. Surely Frank wouldn't keep him late at the ranch on a Friday. If she was going to talk to him before Meira got back, he'd better hurry.

The slam of a truck door sent her to watch the big man stride up the flagstones, leaning as if he walked against a steady wind. Everything about him spoke of strength and solidness, like the trunks of majestic trees. Everything about him was dark and silent, like the gathering of thunderheads before a storm.

Meira had told her once that he was half Hopi Indian. Frank said they'd taken to calling him Kodiak at the ranch because of his size. Jo had never asked him about his life, and he seemed to know not to ask her about hers.

What was important was that they'd become friends.

"Afternoon, Guacamole."

Out of habit, she gave him her usual glare at the silly nickname before she opened the screen door.

He had to take off his hat to duck through the doorway. Hair the color of obsidian brushed his collar.

"I'm glad you're finally here. Meira had to go for a sitting, but the paintings are ready." She led him into the studio. "She should be back soon."

The furnishings of the room seemed to diminish in his presence, Meira's easels looking like spindly aspens in the shadow of a redwood. Kody was swarthy and taciturn, with a scowl she'd heard stopped fights, a demeanor that could bring rodeo clowns to their knees. A man not to be pushed.

But the cats knew better. Flannigan raised his head, and she couldn't help but grin as he rolled to his feet and jumped down, crossing the floor at a trot to beat the other cats to Kody's legs.

"Hello, old-timer." He knelt to greet him and the five other cats who appeared like spirits out of ether.

The cats knew a Ferdinand when they saw one.

"Meira left six paintings for you to check. They're over here." She walked to the easel, embarrassed that she was stalling. Kody had consulted on Meira's paintings before. He knew the procedure.

All day she'd waited to talk to him, but now she couldn't bring herself to mention Trey. She'd seen Kody study him at the stables the other morning. What if he agreed with all her suspicions?

He followed her to the easel where the first painting rested. From the pocket of his crisp Western shirt, he pulled a small pad and the stub of a pencil.

"Well... guess I'll go now." She stepped back. Kody would probably tell her not to trust Trey, and he had a whole lot better judgment than she. She carried too much emotional baggage to think clearly, and Kody had that uncanny ability to see things.

She watched him study Meira's vivid interpretation of an ogre kachina, make a few notes and put the canvas down.

"The rest are stacked against the easel." She backed away another step.

He nodded, setting the next painting into place. "You made a long ride with the cowboy."

She wanted to hug him for helping her, but instead she breathed a silent sigh of relief. "Too long, Kody. He wants to buy Meira's land, start a *camel* ranch. He's from *Vermont.* I can't stop wondering whose dream the ranch will fulfill."

Kody abandoned the painting to consider her with those dark eyes, his silence making her all the more aware of how piecemeal her ramblings were. He always seemed to look more deeply into things, always saw what she didn't.

"He has a son," she added. "A five-year-old son." A little boy with need in his eyes.

She had to look away then, afraid Kody would delve into her own eyes and see what Trey had left behind. Desire—like nothing she'd felt for Jason. A foolhardy longing to trust him.

Fear.

"But he hasn't come around for two days. He hasn't contacted Meira. I don't know what to think." She didn't know what to feel. She wanted to believe Trey wouldn't hurt Meira. She wanted to believe he wasn't like Jason.

Kody moved the painting aside and put up another. "Ah, Tawa, the Sun Kachina. Well-done."

His ebony gaze settled on her again, offering the peacefulness of a clear night sky. "It is said, those who don't touch fire never know its strength." He waited for the space between heartbeats before returning to the painting.

What was Kody telling her with these words? They were more words than she remembered him ever stringing together before. Was he quoting some kind of Indian wisdom? Or was he trying to bring her to her senses kindly? She'd touched fire before. Fire burned.

A solid knock shook the screen door. Impatiently she glanced beyond him. Meira hadn't said anyone else was coming this afternoon. Whoever it was had terrible timing.

Silhouetted behind the screen, a figure stood, with slanted shoulders and the shape of a Stetson on his head. Jo's hand rose involuntarily to her chest, failing to slow the sudden quickening of her heartbeat.

Her imagination had short-circuited, that was all. It was the mailman. A customer inquiring about a portrait. A passerby whose car had broken down...whose horse...

Reluctantly she moved to the door, jamming her hands into her jean pockets to keep from checking her hair. Holding her breath.

The screen swung open with its usual complaint just before her heart collided with her ribs. Her imagination simply wasn't this good. "Trey! What are you doing—?"

"Jo? What the hell are you—?"

"I *live* here," she said. He was all taut jaw and tight mouth and deeply etched confusion, and even though she'd sworn she'd never see that face again, she was glad to see him now.

"You live *with* Meira? I thought—"

"My apartment's in the back. She's not home, so I'm—"

"I'll come back later." He stepped away, his eyes dark and cool, like evergreen under snow.

"Trey, look out, you're going to run into—"

But it was too late. Meira sidestepped just in time to catch the sleeve of Trey's faded denim shirt.

"Careful, young man. I don't think I want the weight of those boots on my foot." She peered up at him. "Why, Trey." A smile engulfed her round features, and a bit of a challenge lit her eyes. "I've been wondering when you'd show up."

Meira *did* know him. All of Jo's suspicions shoved forward, like a herd on the verge of stampede.

"Aunt Meira?" Trey murmured.

Jo watched in shock as he stared down at the plump little woman in the aqua caftan, her henna curls haloing her delighted face.

"*Aunt* Meira?"

Ignoring Jo's question, Trey bent to swing her land-lady into a huge bear hug.

Meira beamed and patted Trey on the shoulder as he set her feet back on the floor. "I should have told you, Jo, but I wanted Trey to come here on his own."

Jo squared her shoulders and drew herself up to her full five feet nine inches, just in case this Vermont char-latan playing at cowboy still held any illusions about her being a sweet—kissable—little schoolmarm.

"No, Meira, *Trey* should have told me. Why didn't you tell me, Trey? Wait. Don't answer. I don't need to know. This is between you and Meira. You and your *aunt* Meira."

She turned to leave, to put Trey out of her life—for good this time. But Meira blocked the door. Spinning back into the room, Jo almost collided with Kody where he stood in front of the easel. His questioning eyes watched her.

"Trey, I think you owe Jo an explanation," Meira said.

"I don't want any—" She saw Kody's thick brows rise, heard again his words. *Those who don't touch fire never know its strength.*

If she didn't hear Trey's explanation, she might not know how much of a threat he really was. Meira was clearly happy to see him, but she didn't know a thing about his client. And she obviously wasn't ready to consider her nephew a villain in hero's clothing. Even if Jo did.

Just because Trey was Meira's nephew didn't mean her dream was out of danger.

Chapter Six

> *Miss Jenny wasn't sure just how Chaps did it,*
> *but somehow he sweet-talked her right up onto*
> *that wagon seat. Took her ridin' and told her the*
> *most outlandish story she ever did hear. 'Bout*
> *how his aunt left his family of Eastern city*
> *slickers years ago, jest like he did, 'cause nei-*
> *ther of them ever did fit in. The family dis-*
> *owned her when she went out West, but he*
> *finally tracked her down. Seems the dear widow*
> *Abigail was his long-lost kin.*

"So how is your father, Trey?" Meira asked.

"He's...different...since Mom died."

Jo stopped in her steady retreat toward the door of
Meira's studio. The conversation had suddenly taken on
a whole new aspect. Somehow she'd missed something or
forgotten something that hovered just beyond her grasp.

"Jo told me about your mother, Trey. I'm sorry."

She swung around to stare at Meira. "I didn't tell you..." But it came to her then that she had. She'd told Meira about a client who had lost his wife.

"Mr. Shelton is your *father?*" She saw Trey wince and look beyond as if calculating the distance to the door, the same escape she'd been trying for. "*He's* the wealthy Eastern tycoon?" She should have known.

"Shelton *Covington,* Jo. Trey is going to tell you all about him, aren't you, Trey?" The timbre of Meira's voice was, as usual, more command than question. Sliding an arm around each of their waists, she herded them to the door. "You and *I* will talk later, young man. Right now Kody and I have work to do."

The screen door gave voice to Jo's resistance, and she let it clap shut behind her, wishing that giving it a good solid slam was acceptable for a grown woman. Wishing Trey would march his Vermont-cowboy tush right back down the sidewalk and leave.

Instead he fished in the pocket of his black leather vest and held up a key. "Jeep's out front. Let's go where we can talk."

He wasn't extending an invitation. He *expected* her to go, even though she could feel his reluctance as clearly as her own. She struggled with the urge to march away, to make her escape to the safety of her apartment. It would be nothing but pure folly to stay and hear his story.

"I'm not going anywhere, Trey. I'm...not leaving my own turf."

Hadn't she learned anything from Jason? She shouldn't waver like this, shouldn't allow herself to be swayed by that swagger, that compelling self-assurance that was clearly a part of Trey—whether he wore a Stetson and boots or not.

"Seems to me *all* the turf around here is yours...except the inside of my Jeep and those two hunks of property out there in the wilds of New Mexico."

There was none of the usual wry humor in his eyes, only a flash of anger before his gaze slipped to her lips. As if to remind her that her own turf wasn't much good at protecting her from his kiss.

He raised his hat and dug a hand back through his hair before he settled into an impatient slouch, thumbs hung in his pockets. "Okay, Jo, you call the shots."

"I'd prefer a hanging, but I don't want to clutter up Meira's trees."

That brought a squint of surprise, no more than she experienced herself. This was hardly the time for humor, even if she did wish it could take the chill from his eyes.

"Right here will do," she finally said. "There's a picnic table in the back. Maybe you can pretend it's a banking conference room." She turned to the lilac-lined path at the side of the house and wondered if he'd follow. Seeing his impenetrable frown, she wasn't sure she wanted him to.

"All right, Jo. Let's get this over with."

He took the steps that told her he'd stay and followed her toward the back. Nothing about him suggested he'd given in. Only the crunching of their boots broke the tension-filled silence.

"Trey, why didn't you tell me you were here for your father? Or that Meira was your aunt?" For a moment she wondered if he'd answer.

"Meira and my father are like the Hatfields and the McCoys. They haven't spoken in years." He paused as they came in sight of the table. "I thought getting word to her through you might start her thinking about reconciliation."

"But you lied, Trey. You used me." Jason had done the same thing.

Trey's chin rose a fraction. He looked stubborn, and proud...and guilty as hell. But his gaze locked with hers. "I didn't lie to you, Jo. My sister calls it a sin of omission. It won't happen again."

He reminded her of the hotheaded adolescents she'd told to look her straight in the eye and take their punishment honorably. Behind Trey's hard pride she glimpsed regret—and a healthy portion of the honor she'd tried to teach. Unaccountably she wasn't surprised.

But she'd let herself get entangled before by a man's "sin of omission." The thought sent a shiver up her spine, sent her striding away from him to the table. She wouldn't let that happen again.

"I thought family feuds were the stuff of daytime TV." She straddled the end of the bench, seeking distance and a quick avenue of escape.

Instead of sitting, Trey paced the hard-packed ground at the opposite end. "I never understood it, either. But I think my father has decided to end it. That's why I'm here."

Was it really? A wealthy divorced man with a young son and a dream he'd never outgrown? All of it pointed to a hidden agenda. She *had* learned that much from Jason.

"Meira is the most accepting person I've ever known, Trey. She won't even kill spiders. I can't imagine her feuding with her own brother."

"Brother-in-law. Meira married my father's brother, Cliff. Until I was ten, all I knew was I had this terrific aunt out West whose friends were real cowboys and Indians."

It must have been memories that made the taut lines around his eyes ease. Jo forced herself to look away.

"After my grandfather died, my mother told me the story."

She should get up and leave, before she became involved in the rattling bones of the Covington skeletons. Before she got lost in the way the setting sun traced shadows across Trey's appealing face. Especially when he looked so troubled.

Digging in her pocket, she found a cinnamon drop, unwrapped it slowly and braced to open the Covington closets. "And the story was...?"

He actually drew in a deep breath before he settled on the far end of the bench. "It was Thanksgiving... Cliff's freshman year in college. He brought Meira home with him to meet the family. After they went back to school, he wrote that he'd lost the nerve to tell the formidable Covington clan in person. Turned out he and Meira were married. And Meira was pregnant. *Not* necessarily in that order."

"Oh." She couldn't help the soft syllable of shock and was glad to read concern rather than censure in Trey's eyes. "I guess back then, people didn't approve..." Certainly not a "formidable" family with a social image to maintain. "So Clifford and Meira were sort of... disowned?"

She hadn't expected him to smile. The sight caught her breath.

"Actually, my grandfather wanted to haul them home and give them a proper Covington wedding, replete with five hundred guests, a sit-down dinner and the family blessing. He wasn't a condemning man, and he was smitten with the idea of his first grandchild."

The warmth in Trey's face was the same she'd seen when he was with Billy. Trey might be a man whose ends justified his means, but he had a clear capacity for caring.

"Did they accept his offer?"

Just as quickly, his face darkened. "Cliff had already dropped out of school. Signed up for Vietnam."

"He *left?* While Meira was expecting his child?"

"I don't claim to understand his sense of honor. Or my father's sense of responsibility. As firstborn son, he felt he had to maintain proprieties Grandpa Shel never considered important. My father was the one who rejected Cliff."

"Honor? Responsibility? Trey, how could they act like that toward people they loved?"

Trey flexed his hands where they rested on his thighs. "The Covingtons have been respected in Vermont for generations, Jo. With the exception of Grandpa Shel, they've never coped well with square pegs. They don't have much tolerance for mistakes." His face showed no emotion, as if he'd closed down his feelings.

In a wealthy Vermont family, a would-be cowboy probably was considered a square peg, too, she realized. And divorce was *always* judged as evidence of a mistake.

"Grandpa Shel tried to convince my father he was being unreasonable. He even came to visit Meira. She'd come home here to New Mexico to have the baby." Trey let his hands relax on his thighs.

"That's when he bought the land. Told my father he and Cliff were to use it together when Cliff got back from Nam."

"What happened when Cliff came home?"

Trey ran a hand around the back of his neck, tilting his head until his eyes were hidden again. "He didn't."

"Meira's husband was killed in Vietnam before their child was even born? Before his family gave them a chance?" The shock and injustice of it swelled inside her.

Suddenly she realized something more. "Meira never told me she had a child."

"She didn't. She lost it shortly after she learned about Cliff."

His quiet answer wielded a painful impact. First Meira's husband, then her unborn child. Jo knew something of loss, but nothing this total, this absolute. She couldn't bear to think how much Meira had suffered.

"But Grandpa Shel kept coming to visit. When I was old enough, he brought me along."

He looked up then, and she could see he'd moved on to happier memories.

"Wasn't your dad going against his *responsibilities* to let you visit?" She knew she shouldn't attack Trey. He'd been no more than a kid, perhaps no older than Billy. But she had to put this anger somewhere.

"I don't think my father was aware of where we were going, not until I was old enough to start asking questions. I was ten when he told Grandpa Shel he was sending me to summer camp. We stopped talking about Aunt Meira then."

A father who wasn't aware of his son's trips? Somehow firing more anger at Trey suddenly seemed pointless—or heartless. "Then you haven't seen her since you were ten?"

"I was eighteen at Grandpa Shel's funeral. In his will, he left half the land to my father and half to Meira. After my father saw her there, it seemed like the silence between them just deepened. It's been only in the last year he's shown signs of yielding.''

Why was it when Trey spoke of his father, the fondness he'd shown for the rest of his family changed? To respect? Maybe. The kind that was taught but not earned, the kind given a man called "my father" but never "Dad."

She felt a tug of sympathy, wanted to reach across the space between them and let him know she understood. But caution held her back. After all, Trey wasn't a child anymore.

And something else was wrong with this picture, something that had to do with the evening Meira's face had paled and her eyes had filled with tears.

"Trey, your father's interest sounds more like acquisition than reconciliation to me." Didn't Trey see? His father wanted the land for his own purposes. He hadn't cared about Meira's feelings when he'd rejected his brother, and he had no more reason to care about her dreams now.

"It's an opening, Jo. It's a way to get them talking."

And Meira had agreed to talk. She'd even asked how Shelton Covington was doing. She was too kind and trusting to perpetuate a feud, especially when a little boy she'd cared about had grown up and come to see her.

Heaven help Meira when she saw Billy. She wouldn't stand a chance.

Any hope Jo might have been harboring slipped away as she studied Trey across the miles of differences between them. If only he were what he appeared to be, the self-reliant cowboy, trustworthy and true. She wanted him to be a man of honor and truth. More than anything she wanted to believe Trey was one of the good guys.

But she was afraid.

He was a rough-edged square peg in a family of smoothly polished bankers. Would he let his own sense of honor be worn away to fit in?

"Trey, I don't believe that's why you're here." And she didn't want to fend off any more of his charm. She pushed up from the picnic table and hurried away to her apartment.

Stealing around the back of Meira's house in the dead of night with a bouquet of flowers in one hand and a bag of candy in the other is really pushing it, Covington. Raising the fine art of black-sheep behavior to new levels. Trey paused in the shadows, feeling like a bad impersonation of the Pink Panther and wishing his ankles would quit hurting. It wasn't easy to sneak in cowboy boots, especially along a sandy flagstone path. But risking arrest for skulking was a whole lot better than facing Meira's "You and I will talk later, young man." More to the point, he didn't want Jo hotfooting it out of there if she heard him coming.

Deciding not to see her again had been a monumental waste of effort. He had to talk to her...to try to undo the damage he'd done by making the fool mistake of asking her to help in the first place. He'd been right in guessing Jo was a woman who'd take up arms for someone she cared about. He just hadn't expected her to draw her six-shooter on *him*.

But, damn it, seeing her wasn't a wise move, either. A woman just wasn't part of his game plan right now, especially not *this* woman. She seemed to think he really was a panther, ready to pounce and carry off Meira's lambs. Or was it rutabagas? Whatever it was, he'd had enough of women who thought he needed to mend his ways.

Rounding the last of the bushes, he came to a stop just outside an unexpected pocket of brightness, a small courtyard at the back of the house. Muted gold light filtered from a border of glowing paper bags, their candles casting rosy halos on the curved lines of the adobe house.

A welcoming scene. If he believed in omens, he'd sure take this one because he could use all the good news he could get. Since he'd been here in Santa Fe, he hadn't had any more luck with his son than with Jo. Billy was still as quiet as his favorite stuffed turtle, Emory. And just as withdrawn.

Pretty sad state of affairs when a five-year-old would rather go to the movies with a baby-sitter on Friday night than spend time with his dad. Sad didn't come close to describing what Trey felt.

But he'd work on his son tomorrow. Tonight he had to work on himself—and the day-care lady he spent too much time thinking about when he should be negotiating a camel farm.

An unfortunate pair of options. He wasn't in the mood to grin, but he couldn't help it when he imagined the dark-haired woman with the amber eyes competing with fuzzy sloe-eyed beasts. The camels placed a mighty poor second.

Crossing the inlaid stones of the courtyard, he shifted his peace offerings and raised his hand to rap on the door, then stopped the gesture in midair.

Damn. It *was* Friday night, and Jo had the place lit up with *farolitos* like a Christmas welcome. Probably in anticipation of that "boyfwend." The guy might be inside with her this very minute.

And here *he* stood, as nervous as a kid on his first prom night and feeling just as sophomoric. There was nothing for him to do but knock and get it over with.

The sight of her slender figure behind the screen shouldn't have raised his pulse rate—or the local temperature. He wasn't here for courting, for crying out loud. He'd come to tell it to her straight; let the chips fall where they may.

"Trey?" Surprise shifted quickly to concern in the light that touched her face. "What are you doing here?"

"Are you alone? I mean, I hope I'm not interrupting anything." He saw her dark brows rise slowly and felt another expletive building. "Here. I brought you these." He held out the fat blooms of tiny purple flowers and the red polka-dot bag of candy.

The screen door swung open reluctantly. He stepped back, inviting her to join him outside, and saw her glance from the flowers to the bushes beyond. The courtyard was surrounded by the very same fragrance.

Remember, you're a Covington. The thought came back in a rush. If he'd followed his mother's advice, he'd have brought designer chocolates and long-stemmed red roses.

Jo hugged herself, combing a hand through tousled hair as she tilted her head to peer up at him.

"Why?"

In the loose green sweater, she looked small, almost fragile. And short. Glancing down, he saw that she was barefoot. She reminded him of a winsome kid who'd just awakened from a nap. She looked all sleepy-eyed and vulnerable, as if she'd been spending the evening with a good book. Alone.

Well, damn, he didn't need this. He didn't want to be wondering why. How was he going to act trustworthy and true if she looked so tempting?

"Because I thought you'd like them." The sentiment came out rougher than he'd intended, but it was honest. He'd spent more time deciding on these things for Jo than he had on his first-anniversary present for Cheryn. He really had wanted to please Jo. The realization didn't help his humor.

Jo opened the bag, releasing a spicy scent that played havoc with his memory.

"Cinnamon." She actually smiled at him then.

He felt as if she'd just chosen him the damn prom king as he watched her slip a piece of the candy into her mouth. He couldn't help but remember the same seductive O of her lips just before he'd kissed her. Couldn't stop himself from wanting to taste her again.

"I do like them, Trey, but you didn't answer my question."

Truth in advertising, that was why he was here. He took off his hat and held it with two hands in front of him.

"Fact of the matter is, I wanted to sweeten you up. So you'd give me a bit more time. You left mighty quick this afternoon, and I hate an unfinished story."

He tapped fingers silently on the brim of his hat, waiting to see if she'd play along with his half-baked cowpoke act. Almost missed the whisper of curiosity that flitted across her face and was gone.

"You don't have to bribe me to—"

"Good. Then come set with me a spell." He took her arm and led her to the carved wooden bench at the side of the door, steeling himself against her warmth, fighting the urge to scoop her up and hold her on his lap so she couldn't run away again. Too bad the bench didn't have more in common with the narrow seat of a Conestoga wagon.

She curled away from him into the corner, hugging her knees, and watched him from those big guarded eyes.

Dropping his hat on the other end, he settled beside her bare feet, then couldn't stop looking at the bright pink of her toenails. For some reason, the silly color unsettled him all over again.

How was he going to convince this woman? A woman who slipped in mere seconds from the skittishness of a dove to the feistiness of a blue jay. A woman who painted her toenails the color of flamingos. What other colors did Jo have hidden behind those clouds that filled her eyes?

He pulled his gaze away, refocusing on a cluster of white flowers in a pot shaped like a goat—with a smile on its face! Another of Jo's private whimsies.

Damn. He scrubbed a hand around his nape and forced himself to relax, to stretch his arms along the back of the bench. He hadn't come here to discover rainbows and fancies. The only problem he intended to solve had to do with two plots of land and a family feud.

But he'd have to start off easy if he was going to chase away her caution.

"Remember what I told you about my client, Jo? Silver spoon, country club, family bank and—"

"You mean the client you just happened not to mention was your father? The one related to the woman you neglected to tell me was your aunt?"

So much for persuasion-lite. "Hey, teach, wasn't it Mark Twain said something like, 'mainly he told the truth'?"

"He also described an ambitious and picturesque liar." There was gotcha-satisfaction written across her face.

"I should know better than to challenge a teacher. But just for the record, my parents were barely married when Meira was widowed, so I don't think she's really my aunt. Does that let me off the hook even a little?" He wasn't above pleading if it would get her to keep playing.

She shook her head, her hair glistening mahogany and russet in the gentle light. He resisted the urge to stretch out a finger and touch it, but he didn't want to scare away the reluctant humor around her mouth, the lingering curiosity in her eyes.

"Like I said before, you're a hard woman, Miss Jo." Her unwilling smile practically obligated him to tease. "But I digress from finishing my story.

"I want to tell you more about my alleged client, also known as my father. He's really not as bad as it might have sounded. He *is* a numbers man—by the books and all that—but he's also honest and hardworking. He was a devoted husband, and he gave his kids all the advantages. Even me."

He'd intended to make her smile, but he wasn't prepared for sharp scrutiny. Whatever it was she'd reacted to, he had her undivided attention. Now all he had to do was sell her. After which he'd go out and secure world peace.

"It's just that he's... a doer, Jo, not a dreamer. And he doesn't understand people who are. Like you and me."

Her back stiffened, reminding him a little of a spooked young filly. Was she bucking being called a dreamer? Or was it because he'd lumped her in the same herd with him? He wasn't even sure *she* knew.

"That means he'll *do* his camel farm without giving a thought to Meira's dreams, right, Trey?"

Her resistance suddenly sounded a whole lot more like accusation, but he decided to ignore it. "A year ago I might have agreed, but since my mother's death, he seems to be discovering a few dreams of his own."

"So you're going to win favor by making them come true."

"I always suspected teachers were clairvoyant." He tried not to look at her, but the lure of her startled silence and those surprised eyes destroyed his willpower.

"The thing is, firstborn sons are supposed to march dutifully along in their father's footsteps. At least that's the Covington expectation. But it seems like I always end up marching to the proverbial different drummer. That's been . . . pretty disappointing to him. I think he secretly believes I'm a foundling.

"Now, all of a sudden, he's seeking me out." He paused to capture her gaze. "He wants my help, Jo."

He saw her struggle between resistance and compassion. "You can call it what you want—but I consider it a chance to build a bridge. But I won't do it at Meira's expense."

She turned away from him then, her profile etched in the glowing light of the lanterns. For a moment he thought she wouldn't answer. When she looked back at him, he couldn't read her face anymore.

"What about your own dream, Trey?"

A voice that soft shouldn't be able to pierce a hide toughened by years of not fitting in.

"My own dream? What are you talking about?"

Chapter Seven

Chaps invited Jenny and the widow Abigail on a picnic, and she should have known the little boy would be there, too. She should have known he was Chaps' son, 'cause he was the spittin' image of him. That little boy looked up to Chaps like he was Buffalo Bill Cody. He thought his daddy was the best cowboy in the whole wide world, and he wanted to be jest like him.

"What about the dream you never outgrew, Trey?" Jo unwound from the bench and padded across the inlaid stone of the courtyard, away from the aura of Trey's magnetism. Unfortunately all her mixed-up feelings just followed right along, like rambunctious kids at the daycare center, bumping and shoving, trying to capture her attention.

"I would assume being a cowboy includes running a ranch." She knelt beside a darkened paper bag and struck a match, then touched it to the wick of the candle inside.

If only she could shine light onto Trey's heart as easily. She'd like to see if it were pure gold as he wanted her to believe or just highly polished brass. The problem was, Trey's candor was too disarming. She couldn't risk being unarmed around that aw-shucks cowboy charm.

"That was the dream of a boy, Jo."

She hadn't heard him move from the bench, but she could tell he'd come nearer, dangerously nearer. The cool night air felt suddenly charged with his presence.

He was waiting behind her, she knew just as surely as she knew she shouldn't stand up, shouldn't chance another close encounter with this man who made her smile in spite of all her mistrust. Who made her feel things she hadn't known she could feel. But she couldn't seem to help herself.

Rising, she turned to face him. "Then why are you . . . ?" Like the blaze of the match, heat flared in the space between them. "I thought you..." Her voice sounded inexcusably breathless.

His head tilted and he brushed her lips with his, filling her with bright astonishment. The gentleness of his mouth fanned sparks into licks of flame that danced through her, leaving her weak. *Mustn't let this happen,* whispered in her mind, and she felt him clasp her arms as if he'd heard. She tried to pull away, she really did, but somehow her willpower seemed to melt, like the candles of the *farolitos.*

His mouth coaxed her softly, and she wanted to resist, but her hands knew better, moving apart from the red-alert signals issuing feebly from her brain. Against her will, she let her palms rest on the front of his leather jacket, felt its smooth texture beneath her fingertips, absorbed his heat through its softness. Her fingers tingled as if she played with fire.

She inhaled the overpowering scent of leather and sage and masculine heat, and when his mouth closed over hers, she tasted a musky richness that was chuck wagon coffee and wide open ranges and star-jeweled sky. He kissed her then, holding her close, shaping his mouth to hers, filling her with a flame more sweet and burning than she'd ever known.

Crickets stilled. The whole of the velvet night fell silent as she kissed him back. Sliding her hands under the lapels of his jacket, she drew closer to him, all but lost in the wonder of what he made her feel.

Until something brushed against her legs accompanied by an inquiring mew.

"I hope that's not an attack cat," Trey murmured in the vicinity of her ear, sending warm tingles skittering down her neck and making the volume of her alarm soar.

Flannigan. Emissary of reality. He was what finally made her step away. "He's my conscience." And he'd shown up in the nick of time. She scooped up the big tabby and held him against her chest, much too aware of the smoke in Trey's eyes and her own trembling, both fading more slowly than a glorious New Mexico sunset.

"Ah, Jiminy Tomcat. Should have recognized him." Trey reached to scratch a ragged ear. "And I'm Pinocchio. How's my nose, Jo?"

She couldn't resist looking, though she bit her lip to stall another unwanted smile. Recklessly she studied the straight symmetry, the clean-cut angles of his face. Those mellow eyes, that humor that teetered between teasing and temptation, were more than she could handle.

Hugging Flannigan like a shield, she stepped farther away, out of the dangerous circumference of Trey's aura. "I don't think it grew." Suddenly she wanted more than anything to believe he told the truth.

"Will you support me with Meira, Jo?"

He asked so straightforwardly, so gently. His head barely tilted to one side, and his light-tinged brows inclined over eyes as lucid as a forest reflected in a clear mountain lake.

"Trey . . ."

Flannigan mewed, interrupting her indecision, calling up that faint sense of foreboding. Could she trust him? *Should* she trust that Trey wasn't the self-serving person Jason had been? But—if she looked into her own heart—could she really oppose the possible mending of a family feud?

"Okay. I won't interfere. As long as Meira tells me she's satisfied with the way things unfold. That's all I can promise."

The cat twisted out of her arms with a parting yowl that prodded her apprehension. What was her furry feline conscience trying to tell her?

"I'll take that promise, Jo."

A smile like Trey's could cure the common cold, she mused, although it didn't do a thing to overcome her uneasiness. She watched him stride to the bench where he swept up his Stetson. Shoving fingers back through the swatch of gold-tipped hair, he settled the hat into place.

His boot steps resounded with a satisfaction that made her wonder if she'd just made another huge misjudgment in character.

"I'll see you tomorrow, Cinnamon."

He was unsettling and tantalizing. He made her want to laugh. She'd be out of her mind to have any more contact with him.

"I have to work tomorrow."

"I know. I bought your afternoon trail time. I want to take Billy out to see the land."

"Kody, you have to take my schedule this afternoon." Jo followed him into the stables wishing she didn't feel quite so much like a puppy trailing at his heels. "I'll work for you next Friday. I'll do your stable cleaning on Sunday. I'll—" She nearly ran into him when he stopped to check the latch on a stall door.

"Why?" He continued to examine the bolt.

"I wish it didn't take you so long to get to the point." She saw the subtle shift at the corner of his mouth and knew that was more smile than most people ever prodded from him.

"I just need a change, that's all." A change from a man who used money to get what he wanted, even if it meant buying out a whole tour group. "I'm not up to dealing with tourists today." Or a remote little boy with needs she couldn't fulfill. "I'm getting burned out."

"Burned?" There were multiples of meanings in Kody's measuring black eyes.

For once, she hated it when he showed that rare amusement. "Right, smart aleck, as in touching fire. All it does is burn."

Last night, Trey hadn't answered her question about his dreams. But he had kissed her. Every time she thought of it, she tingled with a delicious warmth...and suspected she was well on her way to getting burned.

He hadn't used a very original form of diversionary tactic—fighting the fire of her afternoon anger with his own kind of fire. But it had worked. Absolutely. He'd got what he wanted from her—a promise to stay out of his way.

And that's exactly what she intended to do.

Kody's gaze strayed beyond her. "Not like you to avoid a few sparks, Guacamole."

"Sparks?" She didn't even want to know what prompted the allusion.

"We need a pint-size horse for the young rider here, Miss Jo."

Sparks—the kind that zinged through her veins at the sound of Trey's smiling voice. She turned then, because facing him and his pint-size sidekick seemed a whole lot easier than braving Kody's knowing eyes.

She should have known better. Trey *was* smiling, that cocky half grin that was more high spirits than arrogance. Just the sight of him set her heart thrumming. But the flutter gave way to outright tenderness when she saw Billy trying to match his short-legged stride to Trey's.

Trey and his shadow. Just another version of the specters that had returned to torment her dreams last night. Worst of all, she knew what she'd find when Billy raised his head. Hurt. Need. Hungry admiration for a father who wasn't there when he was needed.

One of the lost boys. Just like Danny Harcourt.

She couldn't do this again.

"We have a Welsh pony, but you can take my Indian pony if he's used to a bigger animal."

Such an abundance of words from Kody broke through her thoughts. Rooted in apprehension, she watched the two men size each other up.

"Kody, isn't it?"

He nodded, accepting the hand Trey offered.

"Trey Covington. My son, Billy."

Kody's grave expression didn't change as he shook the boy's small hand, stuck forward in a gesture that mirrored his dad's.

"He moved up to a small Connemara this year, so I think your horse would be better. Thanks for the offer."

Kody touched the brim of his hat. "The horse's name is Kalataka, Billy. It means 'warrior' in the language of the Hopi. You can call him Taka. I'll saddle him and meet you at the riding ring. You'll want to get acquainted."

Outside, Jo watched Kody and Trey help Billy onto the diminutive Western horse; she was still amazed at the quiet man's lengthy speech—and his acceptance of Trey.

"Ready to ride, podnah?" Trey patted his son's leg.

Billy's frown took on a grim determination as he nodded. Jo couldn't help a rush of compassion for the brave little boy, or a reluctant softening toward Trey when she saw the pride that shone on his face.

Reins in bronzed hands, Kody led boy and horse around the ring, leaving Trey to close the gate and join her outside the one-rail fence that encircled the track.

"Your friend is good with kids, Jo. Billy was looking forward to this. Got to wear his new jeans and boots."

All her hard-earned defenses slammed back into place at his tome of satisfaction. If Trey chose to relate to his son with expensive little cowboy outfits and privately guided trail rides, it wasn't her concern. It wasn't her place to get involved in his parenting.

She kept her attention on Kody, saw him hand the reins to the boy and continue to walk beside the horse. "He rides well for his age," she ventured, seeking the safe ground of casual conversation.

"He's been taking lessons since he was three."

seem like a giant beast. She wondered if Trey recognized the price Billy paid to please him.

Despite of all the defenses she could muster, her empathy was growing for the little boy. Right along with an unwanted attraction to his father.

But *she* wasn't willing to pay the price for that kind of involvement.

What was impressing Billy the most? Trey wondered. He scanned the countryside, trying to see it through the eyes of a five-year-old. Big outcroppings of stone looking like fortresses? High magenta mountains bigger than the biggest buildings?

"How 'bout those mountains, Billy? Not like the little bumps back home." He saw his son turn away, was caught in Jo's quick questioning glance.

Bad choice of comparisons, Covington. Billy had called home "Mom's house" ever since Trey had moved out. It hurt to know he'd caused his son to make that kind of distinction.

"We had sofa pillows for breakfast." Billy's little-boy voice sounded hopeful as he squinted up at Jo.

Such hesitant words coming from his son, the kid he used to call Chatterbox. But at least he was talking. That was worth a glimmer of hope.

"*Sopapillas*, Billy. Remember I told you it was a Spanish word?"

Billy stared straight ahead, but Trey didn't miss the upward tilt of his chin. He sought Jo's gaze and found a strange mix of censure and sympathy there.

"Did you have them with honey or powdered sugar?" she asked, her sharp glance a caution to Trey.

Billy hesitated. "Honey. They were sticky. But I liked them."

"What else did you do this morning?" she asked gently.

The lengthening silence bothered Trey. "Billy...? Ugh!" He clapped his hand to his chest. Jo's quick frown made her point more clearly than if she'd shot him. "Okay, Teach, I promise not to interrupt again."

He could see her struggle to hold the scowl.

"Good," she retorted. "*Your* turn to talk, Billy."

He looked up at her as if for assurance. "We saw the Indians."

"You mean downtown on the Plaza?"

Billy turned to look at Trey, but this time he withheld parental input and only nodded.

Hesitantly Billy turned back to Jo. "Uh-huh. We looked at all their stuff."

"Some of Kody's tribe sell jewelry there," Jo offered.

"Is Kody a real Indian?"

"Yup. Half Hopi."

"Cool!"

Trey had to concede that at five, *he'd* probably been more impressed with real Indians than with big mountains, too. He'd let himself fall out of touch with his son this past year, which probably had more than a little to do with Billy's withdrawal.

"Yesterday we saw a..." Again Billy hesitated, looked up at Trey. His silence must have been encouragement enough, because he turned back to Jo. "We saw a big rabbit with horns. Like Rudolph."

"Oh, Billy, you went to Jackalope!"

Billy's face lit at that. "Yeah, Jackalope. Dad got me a present and I got a present for my mom. That's a funny kind of store. They have lots of cool stuff."

"They do."

Billy didn't seem to notice the change in Jo's voice or the sudden sadness in her face. But Trey did. It was the same look he'd seen when she'd talked about teaching, the same fleeting shadows returning to her eyes. He didn't want her to turn away again, not now, not when both she and Billy had begun to open up.

"I took Billy to lunch at Rancho de Chimayo before coming to the stables." He wasn't going to make the mistake of prompting Billy again, but maybe he could lure him into sharing more with Jo. Billy seemed to get through to her a whole lot better than he did. "We got to eat out under the umbrellas."

"I had more...so-pa...pillows, and blue chips and an Indian cookie."

Trey told himself it was only Billy's eager outburst that made the sun seem to brighten, that it had nothing to do with the sound of Jo's delighted laughter.

"That's *good*, Billy. Try again. *So-pa-pee-yas.*"

"So-pa-*pee*-yas. I can talk Spanish, Dad."

"That's great. I'm proud of you, son."

A shy smile crept across Billy's face.

His son's reaction actually startled him. For the first time, Trey understood the power of those words. *I'm proud of you, son.* How he'd longed to hear them from his own father.

He sought Jo's gaze, found her smiling, too. She might claim she wasn't a teacher anymore, but she was teaching him. Those back-patting smiles and knuckle-rapping frowns were qualities she couldn't just shed, any more than she could change the honey color of her eyes. Or the inviting shape of her lips.

His memory slipped to the night before, to the kiss she'd returned as hungrily as he'd given it. A kiss that had fallen in the range of earth-moving.

He hadn't come to New Mexico with earthquake insurance.

And he still didn't understand the puzzle he'd lain awake last night trying to solve. Why did a herd of silly-faced camels, one unsmiling little boy and one seismic kiss all seem inextricably tangled with the question she'd thrown at him?

What *about* his own dream?

She wasn't going to ask again. Trey had told her his dream was only a boyhood fantasy, and she would take him at his word—if she had to stuff a fist in her mouth every time her doubts crept up. Which they were doing more and more the nearer they rode to Meira's land—except that these doubts weren't creeping. They were coming on like a herd of stampeding buffalo.

It was her own fault. She had too vivid an imagination. She could just see clusters of long-legged hump-backed beasts roaming this rolling terrain. She could easily picture Trey mounted on Rocinante, galloping out to round them up. Men like Trey made even impossible dreams come true.

Shaking off the fantasy, she glanced at his stern profile, but the small figure on the horse between them caught her attention.

"Trey." She nodded toward Billy. "Your son is about to fall asleep in the saddle."

He leaned forward to check. "Hey, cowboy?" The sight of Billy's nodding head softened his expression. "Guess he'd better ride with me." Stopping the horses, he handed her Billy's reins.

"I can do it," Billy mumbled, half asleep.

"I know you can, partner." Trey caught his slight body under the arms and swung him up into the front of his saddle.

Billy gripped the saddle horn while Trey shifted to make room.

"You're doing great, son."

Slowly Billy's stiff shoulders relaxed, slouching, little by little, until his slender body rested against Trey's. Jo saw his hands slip from the pommel, saw Trey adjust his weight until he cradled his son between his arms.

"Guess we'd better go back, Jo. He's down for the count."

They turned the horses toward the ranch, and Jo guided Kody's pony to follow at the side. "Too much excitement for one day."

"Too much to deal with all week. All year, for that matter."

The steady *clop-clop* of the horses' hooves amplified in the warm afternoon air, filling the uncomfortable silence that fell between them. Trey's concern touched her in ways she couldn't allow, and she didn't have to ask what he meant.

"He's been more and more withdrawn since the divorce. We used to be good buddies, but now he almost acts like I'm a stranger."

"How often do you see him?" The question escaped before she could stop herself. She bit her lip and swore it was the last thing she'd ask.

"Every other weekend and sometimes during the week, but he's been as withdrawn as his stuffed turtle. He won't even let me hold his hand to cross the street. This is the closest we've been in months." He nodded down to the sleeping form resting against him.

Asleep, Billy could easily be mistaken for an angel, Jo thought—an angel with cowlicks to hang his halo on.

"He doesn't cry anymore. Never. Not even when I know he's really hurting."

Trey looked so troubled. How could she stop her growing concern? How could she keep from letting him in?

"I'd hoped our time together out here would make a difference, but he doesn't seem interested in anything. Not in what we do. Or what we buy. At least, I didn't think he was, until he started telling you. Today's been the first time he's really talked, Jo. Because of you."

Overhead a red-tailed hawk caught the thermals and glided by. A lizard skittered across the ground in front of them, and the horses kept up their steady pace, even though the air felt suddenly chill.

"Trey, little kids tend to relate to a teacher. You just need to spend more time with him. Keep telling him how proud of him you are. He has to believe he wasn't the reason you left."

"I've *told* him he wasn't."

Frustration hovered in Trey's frown, and it hurt her to see it. He truly loved his son, even if he didn't always show it in ways Billy understood.

The sight of the two of them, nestled so close in Rocinante's saddle, was turning her heart to putty. But she couldn't act as go-between again. She'd already learned that she couldn't teach a father how to love his son. Far more painful had been learning she couldn't heal a son's hurts.

They had to work this out on their own.

Jo handed the horses' reins to Trey and jumped down to open the gate to the ranch.

Billy struggled to sit up. "Are we there yet?"

"Almost back at the ranch, bud."

"Can we go see the Indian town?"

"I think we need to get you a good night's sleep before we set out on another adventure. We'll go tomorrow."

Billy leaned forward and looked down at her. "I want Jo to come."

"Oh, Billy, I can't—"

"I happen to know that Sunday's trail guide wears a moustache."

There was enticement in Trey's voice and in that droll smile that warmed his eyes with teasing and sent heat coiling through her limbs.

"And the day-care center isn't open," he added firmly.

She climbed into the saddle and rode ahead with the pony in tow. Trey had buried his anguish so quickly she wondered if she'd imagined it. He was all confidence and cocksure cowboy again.

"Won't you give us your tomorrow, Jo?"

"Please . . ." a small voice added.

If Trey had insisted, she could have stood her ground. But how could she ignore the guileless voice of a five-year-old? How could she refuse a man whose invitation sounded like a song?

Chapter Eight

Miss Jenny had to remind herself that all a picnic was was eatin' outdoors. It was fried chicken and potato salad shared with friends. The widow Abigail was a friend, even if she did make excuses not to come along. And little Butch Marshall and his dad, Chaps, too... they were jest real nice friends. Even if little Butch kept calling her Mum. Even though Chaps kept brushing her hand.

Billy's day. That's what this was to be, Trey reminded himself. He glanced at Jo, hands clasped in her lap, sitting in the Jeep's passenger seat. She'd come along because Billy had asked. He'd encouraged her because Billy opened up around her. And because she showed him how to do better with his son. He'd take whatever help he could get.

All he had to do was to show Billy a good time. And keep Jo's kisses out of his mind.

With a flick, he turned down Wynonna's voice on the radio. "So, Billy, this is the road my grandpa used to take me on when I was your age. To go see the pueblo." He sought his son in the rearview mirror but saw only the top of a tousled, sandy-colored head. "Hey, bud, you're not watching the scenery. There are some pretty awesome rocks out there."

Billy gave a halfhearted glance out the window. From the corner of his eye, Trey saw Jo look in his direction. At least she was reacting to something, though he shouldn't be so pleased at her amusement.

"Bet you didn't know that back in the old days bandits hid out in rocks like those," she challenged.

She'd tossed the bait his way, but in the mirror he saw Billy's head come up for a nibble.

"Bandits?"

"Bet you didn't know there were cowboys named Bill back in those days, either." She threw out another baited hook.

Interest sparked in Billy's eyes, the first he'd shown that morning.

Time to play straight man. "Well, let's see, I knew about Buffalo Bill—" Trey fed the name back to her "—and that guy they called *Wild* Bill."

"Wild Bill Hickok. And don't forget the one who was shot right here in New Mexico—Billy the Kid."

"Billy the *kid?*" Billy leaned forward against his seat belt. "Was he a ban . . . a bad kid?"

Jo turned toward the back. "He wasn't really a kid, Billy. He was just kinda short and not *very* old."

"Why was he shot?"

"First he got caught rustling cattle, and then he escaped from jail. But he'd killed some men, too. One story said he shot twenty-one men, one for each year of his life."

"Wow." Billy peered out the window eagerly now. "Did he hide in those rocks?"

Trey discovered it wasn't easy to show proper gravity in the face of his son's newborn excitement. Jo seemed to be having just as much trouble. He couldn't resist a conspiratorial wink, and was glad to see her answering smile.

"I don't know about those exact rocks, Billy. He was shot at Fort Sumner, and that's pretty far from here."

The mirror framed a face much too serious as Billy worked on all this new information. "My name's like his," he murmured.

Trey knew right away he was about to overreact, but he didn't even try to curb it. "No way, Billy. He was a bad guy. I think we should come up with a new name for *this* Billy, don't you, Jo?" Just as quickly as he sought her help, he turned away from her inquisitive watchfulness.

All right, so he was making a mountain out of a molehill. Throwing rocks at ghosts. Just the same, he wasn't going to let his son identify with some pip-squeak gunslinger who became a legend for going around killing people. Who knew what a kid would make of that nowadays, with all the gangs and guns and shootings that went on?

"How 'bout Billy the Big Boy? Or Billy Buckaroo?" he suggested. Jo's unconcealed amusement made him search for inspiration outside the window.

"Hey, look." The sign across the entrance of the barnlike building read Western Wear, Leather and Hides. "I've got an idea. Hang on." He spun into the parking lot and braked outside the entrance. "Come on, you two."

The dark, oil-rich scent of leather greeted them as Billy and Jo preceded him through the door. He breathed it in, telling himself it didn't matter that the minute he'd stopped, Jo seemed to take giant steps away from them both. He didn't understand why she drew into herself like this, why storm clouds gathered in her eyes just when things were going so well. He didn't like that it bothered him so much.

Searching above racks of vests and jackets, he caught sight of a saleswoman dressed in white leather. She hurried over to help them.

"We need a hat for my son here. A *white* hat."

Billy's serious appraisal reflected from the full-length mirror as he viewed himself in the first hat. He turned a sober face up to Trey. "I like this one."

"Hey, partner, you're just getting started. Can't choose the very first one, you know."

Christmas in June. Watching Billy gave Trey that kind of pleasure, seeing his uncertainty give way to wide-eyed disbelief with each new hat the saleswoman brought. It filled him with a happiness he hadn't felt in a long time.

Jo felt it, too, he could tell. In the face of all that five-year-old eagerness, her efforts to stay solemn were failing, miserably. Whatever battle she fought, she was losing, and he watched with relief as she slid onto the bench next to Billy and helped him settle another hat onto his head. She refused to return Trey's gaze in the mirror, and he knew it wouldn't be wise to explore where his feelings were headed.

Almost a dozen hats lay scattered around the floor, but Billy didn't hesitate. Pointing to a light gray straw with a two-cord black band, he looked to Trey for approval.

The hat was a lot like his own. He wouldn't want to put too much significance in that. "Are you sure that's the one you want?"

Billy nodded. "Can I wear it now?"

"Not yet."

He almost relented at Billy's crestfallen face, but he held out, even managing to ignore Jo's clear disapproval. He insisted the hat be boxed, and he carried it out of the store himself. In the parking lot, he opened the Jeep's back door with the fancy spare tire and set the box inside.

"Would the two of you please stand over here." He arranged them side by side next to the Jeep, ignoring their mutual pout. He made a big show of straightening Billy's aqua collar and almost lost his train of thought when he lifted Jo's hat and saw the sun turn her hair chestnut and cocoa.

"Okay, now, raise your right hands."

Billy looked up at Jo. She shrugged. Raising her left hand, she wiggled her fingers and winked at him broadly.

A devilish gleam crept into Billy's eyes, a sparkle Trey hadn't seen in so long, it brought a sweet rush of gratitude. Following Jo's lead, Billy raised his left hand and grinned. Trey could have hugged them both.

Instead he harrumphed. "I can see you two need a lot of training." He passed down the two-person line, making a production of lowering Jo's left hand and raising her right, remembering too late that touching her generated heat. More than heat. Glowering with mock fierceness, he switched Billy's hands, too.

"This is a very serious occasion, you two. Let's have no silly grins." He grumbled and mumbled, struggling for a scowl that failed to cover his own silly grin. "Now, get ready to be deputized. Do you solemnly swear to maintain law and order and always do good deeds? The answer is 'I promise.' "

"You betcha," Jo answered, crossing her eyes.

Trey replaced her hat at a cocky angle, taking care not to touch her again. Stepping to the back of the Jeep, he removed Billy's hat from the box and returned to stand in front of him. "And do *you* promise?" He raised his brows.

Billy smothered a giggle. "Right on!"

"Excellent." With a flourish, he settled the new gray hat onto Billy's head, setting it at the same cocky angle as Jo's. "I now pronounce you Deputy Jo and Deputy Bill of the Marshal Covington Good Guy Posse." He stuck out his hand.

Suddenly serious, Billy slipped his small hand into Trey's, a gesture so tentative he felt his heart wrench. *I promise, too, my son. I won't let you down again.* He held Billy's hand tightly.

"I'm proud of you, Deputy Bill. And you, too, Deputy Jo. Now let's go look at a pueblo."

"Aren't you going to shake Deputy Jo's hand?" Billy's earnest tone indicated that he disapproved of Trey's oversight.

All he'd been trying to accomplish was a little belated self-preservation... but not at the expense of his son's approval. He tucked in his chin and saluted. "Thank you, Deputy Bill. I'm pleased to see you're on the job."

Stepping to Jo, he held out his hand, saw her struggle with reluctance to disappoint Billy. He recognized another reaction, too, this one more carefully hidden, but the same as his own. Anticipation.

"Welcome to the Covington Posse, Deputy Jo."

Her hazel eyes searched his, questioning what she was committing to. Reluctantly she accepted his hand.

With her hand in his, heat filled him like a fire storm. One errant spark of attraction, that's all it had been, but now it threatened to grow to forest-fire proportions, and he couldn't seem to stop it. Jo stirred feelings he'd forgotten, even in his dreams. Feelings that could leap out of control, because he could see them in her eyes, too.

Jo slid her hand away and steered Billy around the Jeep. "Let's go look at a pueblo, Deputy Bill."

Trey felt her pull her heart out of his reach as well. She was withdrawing into that shell again, just like Billy's stuffed turtle. There was something about him and his son she wasn't willing to accept. Too late to fight it, he knew that what should have been annoyance had already become regret.

"Are we there yet?"

"Almost. Do you want to eat lunch in Taos or at the pueblo?" Trey talked to Billy's reflection in the mirror.

"The pueblo. How much longer?"

"Half an hour." Checking his guesstimate with Jo was a good excuse to check her frame of mind. He was glad to see she'd let herself settle back into the bucket seat, but her eyes still carried those somber clouds.

"Will you tell me a story?"

Billy hadn't asked for a story in a long time. Trey's spirits lifted a little. "Great idea, partner. Let's see..."

His gaze strayed once more to Jo. She'd turned a little toward him, evidence that she might relent enough to join in. That gave his mood an extra boost. He cleared his throat noisily.

"Once upon a time...a long time ago...there was a cowboy named Grandpa Shelton—"

A giggle bubbled in the back seat. "Grandpa *Shelton* couldn't be a cowboy," Billy protested.

"Hey, this is a story, remember? You have to use your imagination." Trey cleared his throat again and savored the smile he saw lurking on Jo's sweet lips. "Now, Grandpa Shelton had a *big* ranch out here in New Mexico, and he had a fine looking herd of...camels."

"*Ca*-mels?" Billy protested again.

"Right. Like in the zoo. And one day a big gang of camel rustlers came, led by that well-known and very pretty bandit, Bad Mad McPherson..." He risked a glimpse at Jo; shot her a challenging grin. "And she and her gang rustled all the camels away."

What started as an indignant set to her mouth tilted toward unwilling curiosity, inspiring him to greater heights with his story.

"The gang hid the camels so they couldn't be in all the zoos and circuses and parades. 'Cause they didn't want kids to have any fun if the gang couldn't have some, too. But then—"

"Here he comes to save the day," Jo sang. "Hopalong Covington's Sunday matinee."

Trey raised a finger and cast her an imperious glance. "*Marshal* Covington, if you don't mind. And don't forget his trusty sidekicks, Deputy Jo and that very famous good guy, Deputy Bill."

"Ah, Deputy Bill, the hero of this story."

"Yes. And Deputy Bill led everyone on a search. They hunted high and they hunted low, under rocks and behind cactus, down prairie dog holes and up in trees. And they finally found those camels—in a big...dark...cave."

He paused to savor Billy's laughter, to relish the humor in Jo's eyes. "Then Deputy Bill drew his super-duper squirt gun and captured Bad Mad McPherson and the whole gang. He told them they could have all the camel rides they wanted if they'd come to work at the ranch."

He turned to Jo. Decided to take the chance. "And Marshal Covington told Bad Mad McPherson she could stop... feeling ... so... sad."

Jo's soft intake of breath made the hair stand up on his arms. She studied her hands, clasped again in her lap, and he wanted to cup her chin and turn her face to look at him. To see if there were any chance she might let go of that sadness.

"And they all lived happily ever after, the end. Are we there yet, Daddy?"

Daddy. His son's unguarded excitement should have made his day. "Five minutes to the pueblo," he announced. But they were nowhere near "happily ever after."

It was becoming achingly clear to him where it was that fuzzy camels, and a little boy in a gray hat, and a sad-eyed woman who tasted of cinnamon all came together. In a dream; a dream he thought he'd outgrown. A dream beyond his reach...because Jo wanted no part of any of them.

Taos Pueblo was tarnished gold adobe layered like soft-edged blocks, stretched out beneath forest green mountains under a sky as blue as a robin's egg. Through the middle of the ancient village, a river rippled and sang, accompanied in the distance by the haunting notes of an Indian flute. Outside aqua-framed doors, round adobe ovens offered up the pungent scent of piñon smoke and the sweet aroma of baking.

Jo couldn't keep her mind on the scenery. She couldn't stop thinking about Trey, this man who'd moseyed into her life like a Texas ranger and threatened to do the same to her heart.

She watched him choose a picnic spot on rocks near the river and thought of sitting next to him, of absorbing his sun-warm scent. She waited while he popped the tops of icy colas, anticipating the brush of his hand against hers. She saw the attention he gave to dividing Indian tacos, to getting Billy settled with his, and her heart softened at his care. She watched him wipe his hands on the square of red handkerchief he pulled from his jeans pocket—and wanted to lick his fingers.

That made her practically scramble to sit on Billy's far side, to busy herself in eating. But she hardly tasted the food for the heat pulsing through her veins. What she needed was a good solid reality check, some cold hard facts.

"So tell me what you do, Trey." She kept her focus on the distant mountains while she ate.

"What I do?"

He sounded amused, but she didn't dare look into those eyes. "When you're not out procuring camel farms for wealthy Eastern tycoons."

"Ah. *That* kind of 'do.' I wondered when you'd ask."

Out of the corner of her eye, she saw him turn to look at her over Billy's head. She could feel the probe of his gaze.

"I work for the bank."

Worse than she thought. Trey's quiet revelation should have hit like a bucket of cold water. Trouble was, the image of him in a suit and tie still included sun-tipped brown hair and eyes the color of piñones, eyes that held laughter like a promise, and a mouth that promised more. And something else—a heart that loved his son. Trouble was, even if his vaults held millions of dollars, this new image left her just as breathless as the old.

"I thought you marched to a different drummer. Why would your father hire a son he's disappointed in?" She was pushing for a fight, she knew, goading him to shoot back and force her behind barricades again.

Instead he patted Billy. "Hey, partner, want another piece?" At Billy's nod, he plopped a triangle of bread and beans onto his napkin, then held one out to her. She took it reluctantly, avoiding his questioning eyes and the glistening juices on his fingers. Feeling her carefully constructed safeguards crumble a little more.

"First Billy wants a story, now you, Jo." His outlandish smile told her he wouldn't accept her battle.

"Preferably one with more facts and less imagination."

"Just the facts, ma'am." He nudged back his hat and deepened one corner of his smile. "Once upon a time, a *looonng* time ago, my father started me out in the mail room. Pretty soon, though, I was 'removed' for making suggestions to streamline the system—ideas that would have cost some up-front money."

Jo concentrated on eating, trying not to react to the boldness of a kid who thought up ways of improving a long-established family business while working in the mail room.

"During college I was a teller—until they found out I'd devised a better system to close out each day...without permission. End of teller career." He grinned.

Trey was proving good to his word because picturing him coming up with renegade programs that overthrew banking tradition required no imagination at all.

"The manager of customer services fired me for what he called harebrained ideas. My father decided he'd better hire me back when the competition started offering some of the services I'd suggested."

She should have known—Trey was a natural maverick.

"By then I had my M.B.A., and I guess he hoped I might mellow with age. He named me vice president of new business development. That's bank lingo for someone they don't know what else to do with—a contrarian with a lot of wild ideas."

It didn't take a mathematical whiz to see that for Trey banking just didn't add up. "Why do you stay?"

His answer was a long time in coming. "It's a job. I like to persuade people. It gives me a lot of time."

"Time for what?" She knew she shouldn't challenge, that she should leave his world and his uneasy place in it alone, because he would go back to it as soon as he finished here. But she couldn't quite ignore the unexpected loneliness in his eyes.

"Time for Billy." He paused as if weighing how much more to share. "Time for my mother while she was ill." Billy looked up then, and that seemed to rouse him. "I ride a lot, and play the guitar. I'm a big hit at family get-togethers." Suddenly his words raced. "Ever heard of the Covington Five?"

"Never."

"Neither has anyone else. My mother was our best fan." With that, he levered up from the rocks, wiped Billy's hands and gathered the remnants of their picnic.

Jo imagined him gathering any stray feelings he might have left exposed.

"Party's over, deputies. Let's go be tourists." Trey raked a hand back through his hair and resettled his hat. Billy stood up beside him and did the same.

Looking up at them, she understood the meaning of bittersweet. Even if Trey chose custom-made suits and silk ties, in his bones, he was a cowboy—independent, self-reliant and just plain cocky. And Billy was fast becoming just like him. They looked as if they *belonged* on a ranch, not in some stuffy old bank. On a ranch audacious enough to suit Trey's creativity. A ranch that raised camels. In New Mexico.

They started with the adobe-style St. Jerome Catholic church, but the minute they emerged into the sunlight, Billy grabbed Jo's hand and Trey's and pulled them along.

"Come *on,* Mom—I mean Deputy Jo. I hear drums."

Her heart stumbled a bit before it fell into the rhythm of the measured beat. To a little kid, "Mommy" was only slightly more habitual than "why." The kids at the day-care center called her that all the time.

Hiding her fluster, she let Billy and Trey tug her into a pueblo shop in search of the native rhythms. Thick-walled and whitewashed, the space was lit only by sunlight. Display cases of Indian crafts lined the walls, and a boom box proved to be the ironic source of the age-old cadences.

Hands at his sides, Billy studied several shelves stacked with drums—cylinders of all sizes painted with animal figures and stretched with smooth, marbled rawhide.

"You can try them." The copper-skinned proprietor handed him a drumstick, its end wrapped in leather.

Billy looked up at Trey.

He nodded. "Give it a try."

As he tapped hesitantly on one of the small octagonal drums, Billy's face lit with delight. He tried a log drum resting on the floor, and it boomed back at him. His grin was pure joy.

"Pick out the one you like, son, and we'll take it back with us."

She should have seen it coming, but she still wasn't prepared for the disappointment. Trey loved his son, but he needed to learn that love shouldn't be meted out in dollars, or hats and drums. Billy warmed up now, as any five-year-old would, making Trey believe he was doing the right thing. But it wouldn't be long before Billy knew the difference between love and money. Before he rebelled against *things*.

"Come look at these, Jo," Trey called.

She didn't want to face him, not until the urge to tell him passed, but Billy was too absorbed in the drums to offer an excuse.

"I'd wager you'll never be round like Aunt Meira, but these still remind me of you."

That drew her over to where Trey studied a collection of ceramic figures—plump-seated women with faces full of contentment, their bodies like giant laps covered with tumbling smiling children.

"They're called storytellers," she murmured.

"Then you must have one."

The familiar offer only deepened her disappointment. "Trey, no. They're more expensive than you realize. I don't want you to spend—"

"Just a little memento... of our day of storytelling."

His casual disclaimer actually hurt, and she hated that it did. He'd called the gift a memento... a remembrance of things past. He was telling her that when all the wheeling and dealing were done, he would leave.

But she wasn't sure, anymore, that she wanted him to go.

Chapter Nine

Goin' home from a picnic was always the sad part, Jenny thought, especially after havin' so much fun. Up on the wagon seat beside Chaps, she held little Butch in her lap and wondered whatever she was goin' to do. Little Butch was slowly creepin' into her heart, and Chaps threatened to steal it right away. But he still wanted to raise cattle. He still wanted his aunt Abigail's land.

The ride home from Taos Pueblo wasn't any easier than the trip going, and Jo didn't want to think about why. She'd been so reluctant to be a part of Trey's day with his son. Now she didn't want it to end.

But she had to stop dwelling on that kind of thinking. "I see a pink rabbit."

"Where?" Billy demanded.

"There, in the clouds." She pointed to the sunset changing the sky to a vast canvas of blazing colors. "Bet you guys can't find any animals."

They did, of course, and even though Trey found an orange camel, she kept right on laughing, declaring Billy's big red pig the winner.

She watched the sun slip below the horizon and listened to the radio offer up a familiar old song about being someone's sunshine. A swell of yearning filled her, for things that could never be with this man and his son. Then Trey began to sing.

His voice matched everything about him—strong and sure and true—a rich, mellow baritone. His song flowed around her like starlight, casting a spell that made her as muzzy as if she'd sipped moonshine.

An announcer interrupted, and Trey turned the radio down. From the back seat, Billy's shy voice lifted hesitantly, starting with "Row, row, row your boat." Trey joined in, softly at first, and Jo couldn't resist singing, too, until they got carried away with "merrily, merrily," which came out "mellory, mellory," and set them all to giggling.

"I'm cold," Billy announced.

"Guess I shouldn't have left the doors off. I didn't think about it getting so cool here in the evenings." Trey flipped on the heater. "How 'bout you, Jo? Maybe we should stop somewhere and pick up some blankets. Real Indian blankets, what do you say, Billy?"

Over her shoulder, Jo saw Billy draw up into a ball and tug his jacket down over his knees. He looked prepared to tough it out in silence. What he needed, she knew, wasn't an expensive Indian blanket.

"Want to come sit with me?"

Without a word, Billy was over the center console and settling into her lap before she could consider the wisdom of her offer. Instinctively she wrapped her arms around his small frame, treasuring his trust as he curled into her, sharing her warmth with him. Finding in his closeness both sweetness and loss.

She mustn't let herself love this little boy.

Trey tapped his fingers on the small round drum Billy still clutched in his hands, keeping rhythm with the new song from the radio. "We'll have to see if we can do something together with your drum and my guitar." He ruffled Billy's cowlicks. "Maybe Deputy Jo will join us."

Billy didn't answer, and she was glad he hadn't jumped at the idea. She watched his small fingers match Trey's tapping, then slow as his body slumped more completely against her. He was falling asleep.

From the radio, Clay Walker sang that he knew what love was. His question echoed in her mind.

What's it to you? she wondered, looking over at Trey, wishing the answer were something different. She saw a man struggling to mend his relationship with his son. Without even thinking, he used money to try to solve problems, to show his love. But money couldn't buy Billy's love, any more than it could Danny Harcourt's. She knew that with a certainty grounded in grief.

Money couldn't buy a woman's love. She'd learned that from Jason, too.

Trey stopped the Jeep smoothly in front of Meira's house and turned off the headlights. Billy didn't stir.

"I hate to wake him," she whispered. But she had to, just as surely as she had to give up this day, with all its illusions, all its close sense of family.

"Let him sleep a minute more." Trey turned to face her in the darkness of the front seat. "Thanks for coming with us, Jo." His voice still held the softness of starlight. "This was the best time we've had together in a year. You made that happen, you know."

"Trey, it wasn't me—"

He placed a finger against her lips, stalling her breath in her throat. "I love this little guy, but I don't always know how to get through to him. You're a good teacher."

"I'm not—"

This time he silenced her with his lips, and what she'd thought was starlight suddenly became starfire. He brushed her mouth with his, so softly, so sweetly she thought she would shatter into a shower of sparkling lights. Wonder and hunger scattered through her like colors from a prism, drawing her inexorably to the end of the rainbow, where his arms waited. She wanted to feel him against her, to draw him to her, to lose herself in the consuming heat of his kiss.

But a sleepy figure murmured and stirred in her arms.

With that, Trey was out of the Jeep and around to help her, leaving her falling through space like a star, hoping the flame would burn out quickly. Leaving her bereft— and sadly relieved.

He held Billy while she climbed out, and together they resettled him, half asleep, into the passenger seat. Trey helped her tuck her jean jacket around him and snap the seat belt, and she fought the lure of stardust each time he brushed against her.

Opening the back of the Jeep, he retrieved the package that held the storyteller gift and slipped it into her hands. "I'll be right back, Billy. I'm going to walk Jo—"

"No," she said, interrupting him too loudly. "You shouldn't leave him out here alone." *She* shouldn't be the reason for leaving him. "Good night. Thank you...for everything."

She all but ran up the flagstone walk, fighting the urge, the need to look back at Trey. Refusing to admit the longing that still consumed her.

God help her, this shouldn't be happening. It didn't matter that Trey made her laugh. It wasn't important that he turned her resistance to stardust. It was inexcusable that she wanted more than just the whisper of his kiss.

She wouldn't let herself fall in love with this man. She wouldn't come between Trey and his son.

Resolutions always seemed keepable in the solitary hours of the night. On the playground of a day-care center on a Monday morning, they seemed as fleeting as the sounds of wind chimes that floated away on the wind. Especially when she saw Billy, sporting his new hat, running ahead of Trey to greet her. Jo wondered if she had even an ounce of willpower left.

"Billy! What are you doing here?" She wasn't sure she wanted to hear his answer.

"Going to school. You weren't here before. Will you play with me today?"

Over his head she saw Trey wave at spectacled little Charlie. He'd absolutely delighted Charlie when he and Billy were here before. Instinctively, she knew that hadn't been their only visit. *Trey had bought Billy a place at the center.*

Bonnie had told her they were full for the summer, but Trey had crossed her palm with enough silver to make an exception. She could tell by Trey's look of satisfaction.

She couldn't blame Bonnie. Earnings from daycare were always meager.

But she could blame Trey. Daycare could easily lead to a private boarding school. The possibility made her shiver.

"Hey, Cinnamon. I brought your jacket. Billy was excited about you being here today. He missed you Thursday and Friday."

Jo braced as Trey handed her the jacket, smiling that lazy half smile. "I'm sure he's found lots of friends to play with." Her cool tone didn't seem to faze him.

"Today's the day, Jo. I'm going to see Meira this morning. Time to start working on the feud. Wish me luck."

"You don't need luck, Trey."

But Meira did. Last night she'd seemed her usual chatty self, asking about their trip to the pueblo, interrogating her about Billy and Trey. But then Jo had asked about the feud.

"Shelton did what he thought was right," Meira had answered. "We all have to do that."

She'd almost sounded as if she were defending Trey's father! That's when it had occurred to her that there might be more to the story. If there was, she didn't want to hear it.

"Come on, Billy. Your dad's got business to do. Let's go find some kids for you to play with." She held out her hand, but he shook his downcast head.

"Stay with me." The appeal was meant for Trey.

"I won't be long, partner. Remember? I told you I'd be back by lunchtime. Come on, Billy, you can play with Deputy Jo now. I have to leave."

Trey's eyes held the same plea she'd heard in Billy's voice.

She didn't want to be a part of this. *You need the job,* another part of her answered. Trey was just a customer and Billy a reluctant child who needed distraction until he made the adjustment.

And camels could fly. Damn.

She took Billy's hand. "Deputy Bill, I need a driver for the wagon, and I think you're just the man for the job." She started walking and was relieved that he didn't resist. "We got a real problem with camel rustling around here, and..." She led him away, keeping up a running chatter.

He only looked back once, but the need that filled his eyes didn't stop Trey from leaving. All Billy wanted was time—to be with his dad, to be assured beyond doubt, beyond deeds, that he was loved. But Trey didn't see that.

And it wasn't her job to tell him. It wasn't up to her to teach a parent how to raise his kid. Trey had to learn to be a father on his own.

Trey kept his word. Because he wanted to dispel that haunting look of disappointment on Billy's face. Because he wanted to appease him for the time he had to take again this afternoon.

Today would be the absolute last time, he promised himself, trying to shake the guilt and not having much luck. He shifted the tub of chocolate ice cream to his other shoulder and strode down the day-care hall toward the sounds and scents of the lunchroom, ignoring the bag of cups and plastic spoons whacking against his thigh in reproach.

All he needed was enough time to talk to his father, to discuss finances and arrange travel and meeting dates. Then he'd pull Billy out of here, and they'd spend the rest of his visitation together.

Stopping in the doorway of the room, he spotted Jo handing out drink cartons to the children at the tables.

He couldn't help but appreciate her smile, the sway of her auburn hair, the soft curves of her lithe figure in the knee-length tan skirt and soft yellow blouse. Better not linger, or his growing heat would start ice cream trickling down his neck.

He'd like to share more days like yesterday with her. Hell, it seemed that every day that went by he wanted to share a whole lot more with her—like kisses that went beyond friendly persuasion. Like the desire he had to tamp down whenever he was with her. Like the cool smoothness of his bed.

She looked up at him then as if she'd felt his caress, and her smile faltered, then fled. She was angry with him for leaving Billy. But there was more—those dark clouds that forecast her withdrawal.

Damn it, he'd spent his whole life knocking around in expectations that didn't fit. His father wanted a traditional heir and successor, not a self-invented iconoclast. Cheryn had wanted weekend golf and country club parties, not campfire sing-alongs and rides in the woods.

He didn't fit Jo's expectations, either, though hers weren't so easy to fathom. But he couldn't repeat the same mistake. He'd be a fool to let his feelings grow, hoping everything would somehow work out. He couldn't put Billy through that again. He couldn't do it to Jo.

Resolve cooled him faster than the barrel of ice cream threatening frostbite to his shoulder. Hefting the container, he searched for Billy and spotted him at a table near the front.

"Ice-cream man," he announced and watched all those animated faces turn. "Ice cream for everyone, compliments of Billy Covington. Where should I dish this out, Miss Jo?"

Excitement rippled through the room, raising the noise level by decibels, bringing teachers to their feet. Trey felt a tug on his sleeve. Billy peered up at him.

"Hey, partner, I brought a surprise. Want to help?"

His serious nod prodded Trey's guilt. "Good. You're in charge of cups and spoons."

"How nice of you to bring a treat for everyone, Mr. Covington. You can set up over here. Jo, will you help?"

Trey recognized Bonnie Carlson, the program director he'd negotiated with last week. Following Jo to a front table, he set the tub in the space she cleared, all too aware of the spicy scent of cinnamon.

Without speaking, Jo took the package of cups and showed Billy how to set them out. "We're ready when you are."

Only then did she look him straight in the eye, and her barely disguised opposition confirmed all his suspicions. But, damn it, he didn't understand why she disapproved.

"You *did* bring an ice-cream scoop, didn't you?"

He smothered another oath. "Does a Swiss army knife have an ice-cream scoop?"

Her deepening frown made clear she wasn't about to be cajoled.

"Lucky for you we have one in our kitchen. I'm sure the kids would love to watch you dig that ice cream out with a plastic spoon."

Miraculously a shiny metal scoop appeared and a semblance of a line formed. Trey escaped into the task of scooping. Jo's sarcasm only sharpened his guilt.

"I had a good meeting with Aunt Meira," he offered, trying another tack.

She didn't answer.

"She says she's willing to talk to my father."

Still no response.

"She's willing to hold up on her plans until she hears what my father has to say."

Silence colder than the ice cream.

"Jo?" Damn it, what was wrong with her? What had he done? All he wanted was to heal a family rift. She acted as if he were going to rob Meira blind.

"I assured her that whatever my father offered would be generous."

With that, Jo whirled away.

"Daddy?"

Billy's small voice was as charged with questions as Trey was seething with frustration. Fiercely he dug into the ice cream.

"It's okay, partner. We can handle this on our own."

Jo stood in the small day-care kitchen and swiped at her cheeks with the backs of her knuckles. Trey Covington was the most blind, misguided, ignorant, oblivious, hardheaded, good-intentioned, kindhearted man in the world. Or else, she was a complete fool. More than likely, both.

How could he be so blind to Billy's needs at the same time he hauled a ton of ice cream in here just to show he loved him? How could he be so misguided as to believe his father would be "generous" with Meira just because *Trey* wanted to mend the feud? How could he make her want to laugh and cry with the same smile?

How could she be falling in love with him?

She was. It was as simple as that. As frustrating as that. As impossible. She'd just have to bury it away, because she was growing to love Billy, too, and she wouldn't be the cause of any more hurt.

Tugging a tissue from a package in her pocket, she snuffled into it. Wiped her eyes once more, and pinched her cheeks to distract from the pink she knew tinged her nose. Then she walked back out into the lunchroom.

The line of children had disappeared, and Trey was talking to Bonnie.

"Did you get everyone?" She looked at Bonnie, afraid if she saw Trey's eyes, the tears would start again.

"I think so. Except you and Mr. Covington."

"I don't think Billy's had his." Jo fought the wobble in her voice.

"And he's the birthday boy," Bonnie exclaimed.

"It's not my birthday. Not till next week." Billy looked more solemn than ever.

"But you *can* have some ice cream today." Trey ruffled his hair, then dipped into the tub.

"Then can we go?"

Jo saw the flash of discomfort on Trey's face, and her heart plummeted further. The look could mean only one thing.

"Well, son..."

"You *said*..."

She could hardly bare to watch. But she couldn't walk away from Billy now.

"I know," Trey said softly. He sounded miserable.

Jo struggled between fury at what he was about to do and heartache for the pain it clearly caused him.

"I have just a little more business, partner, that's all. I promise. Then I'll come get you and we'll—"

"I don't *want* any ice cream. I don't *want* your dumb old promise." Billy turned and ran.

"Billy, wait!"

"I don't want to talk to you."

Jo watched Billy charge out the door and felt her heart tear. "You've got to go after him, Trey. You can't leave him like this."

He turned troubled eyes to her, dark like a forest before a storm. "He won't talk to me, Jo. It's happened before. I thought we'd gotten beyond this, but I guess he still doesn't trust me. Will you look after him till I get back?"

Desperately she looked to Bonnie, Bonnie who belonged with the five-year-olds, who'd been Billy's teacher the past two days. But she was already making her way to the kitchen with the remnants of the ice cream.

Jo straightened, though she felt the weight of impending defeat. "I'll find him, Trey. I'll make sure he's okay and get him back to his class."

She started to say more, to tell Trey it was up to *him* to look after Billy. But she let it go. Trey was too much his father's son, too strongly influenced. How could he change if he didn't understand? The problem wasn't Billy. It was him.

Chapter Ten

*"A mean-lookin' sou'wester was brewin' over-
head when Jed came tearin' into the Dry Goods
Store looking for help to find his lost calf.
Course, Chaps stepped forward and offered to
ride along. Jenny's heart was heavy to see Chaps
go, but she offered to look after Butch while he
was gone. She didn't want that little boy gettin'
caught out there in that storm."*

"So is he nice, Jo?"

Jo didn't look up from filling two more buckets with
feed. She could pretend she thought Adela meant the
hero of their story, but she probably wouldn't let her get
by with that for long.

The slender youngster in the bright red shirt finished
filling the water buckets. "What's his little boy's name?"

"I told you, it's Butch." Hefting the filled buckets, Jo
ducked into the stall.

"You know what I mean." Adela sounded exasperated. "Aren't you going to tell me about them? He's a hunk!"

Not exactly the way Jo thought of Trey, but close enough. She squelched a smile, sure that if she didn't come up with some answers, Adela would hound her the rest of the morning. She didn't want to talk about Trey the hunk. Or about Billy. She didn't want to think about them.

"Okay, I'll answer five questions. You've already asked two, so spend your other three wisely." She waggled a warning finger accompanied by a teacherly scowl.

"Aw, come on, Jo."

"Take it or leave it."

"Oh, all right." Adela followed her to the last stall. "So *is* he nice?"

Jo hesitated. "I guess I'd have to say yes." Trey *was* nice. More than nice. He was thoughtful, and considerate, and fun to be with. Nice to kiss. Damn.

"His son's name is Billy," she added quickly, blocking the direction of her thoughts. She carried the bucket of water into the last stall and hooked it firmly in place.

"Did he...ask you for a date?" Adela's smile wavered between shyness and mischief.

"We took Billy to Taos Pueblo, but I wouldn't call that a date." A date didn't consist of trying to get a little boy to open up. That was exactly why she shouldn't have gone. All she'd managed to do was get more emotionally involved. She didn't want to get more emotionally involved. She didn't want Billy assuming things about her and his dad that simply weren't true.

"Did he buy you a present?" Adela's eyes danced now.

Jo needed to bring this interrogation to an end. She needed to bring the *relationship* to an end, though that was hardly what she should be calling it. "He bought us each a souvenir from the pueblo, that's all."

Something simple and silly would have been more appropriate than the pricey storyteller, even though she'd cherish the love-filled piece of sculpture long after Trey had folded his tent and stolen silently away.

Carrying feed into the last stall, she poured it into the feed bowl and patted the horse before he dipped in. Out in the aisle, she found Adela planted in front of the feed cart, hands on hips.

"Do you *like* him, Jo?"

The question made something deeper than regret creep into her chest. She did like Trey. In addition to everything else she felt for him was the abiding sense that he was a good man. Honorable, and caring.

Somehow she knew he went after what he wanted because he believed it was right. The problem was, he didn't know when he was wrong. Or how badly wrong he was.

"You have to answer my last question, Jo. Do you like him?"

"I'd like to hear the answer to that, too, Cinnamon."

Trey's deep voice sent her heartbeat skyrocketing. He might as well have thrown a string of lighted firecrackers into the stables for all he'd just done to her equilibrium. She whirled around, her pulse in an uproar. "What are you doing here?"

He stood at the stable entrance looking just the way she would always remember him—cocky slouch, hat set low on his brow. But today she could see the square planes of his face, could watch the corners of his wide mouth curl into that tantalizing smile.

Billy stood beside him, a diminutive twin except that he wasn't smiling. There were shadows under his eyes, such a heartbreaking contrast to the devilment that danced in Trey's.

"I thought if we started early, Billy could manage the whole trip. I want him to see his grandfather's land before he gets here."

That made her erratic heartbeat stumble. So it was really going to happen. Meira was going to meet with Shelton Covington—and probably lose her land.

"Fine. I'm sure Kody will be glad to take you out." She threw the scoop into the feed cart and relished the angry clank. "Come on, Adela, let's go."

She marched out of the stables into the overcast gray of the morning . . . and stopped dead in her tracks. Billy and Adela piled up behind her.

Next to the hitching rail, Kody was throwing a saddle across Rocinante's wide back. Taka stood next to him, already saddled, but it was the sight of Dusty that filled her with foreboding. Kody knew she preferred to ride Dusty.

"Horses are ready, Guacamole. Billy, let's get you mounted. Taka's been looking for you."

Jo saw Billy slant a look at Trey, not a childish appeal for permission, but a glimmer of rejection too distressingly familiar. In Danny Harcourt, rebellion had worried her. In a five-year-old, it was frightening.

Billy's exaggerated strides spiked her concern. He stalked over to Kody without waiting for a nod of approval from Trey.

This shouldn't be happening. She didn't want to be part of this.

Trey followed her to the side of the riding ring. "We'll give Billy a little time to get used to Taka again."

Just who did he think "we" was? Who did he think *he* was, cruising in here as big as John Wayne, buying up her time, imposing himself and his son into her life? Into her heart?

She clung to the protection of anger, trying to make it easier for herself—she'd be damned if she'd make it easy for him. In a haze, she saw Kody beckon to Adela and watched the girl start Billy around the ring as Kody strode away to the stables.

"I reserved your whole morning, Jo, so we don't have to hurry."

She'd already suspected what Trey had done, but having it confirmed didn't make her day. Too late, she realized she should have walked away with Kody. "Trey, you can't—"

"And again for Thursday."

For the first time, the sight of his grin sparked real anger. "Why Thursday, too?"

"I made arrangements to bring the five-year-olds from the day-care center to ride. For Billy's birthday."

That just took the air right out of her indignation. She looked over at Billy where he straddled the glossy pony, reins clutched in his fists, his face a tight little knot of resistance. *Oh, Trey. Don't you see?*

She couldn't let him do this. She couldn't bear to see what was happening. She couldn't stay quiet any longer—not while he drove his son farther away.

"Trey, we need to talk."

"I'm right here, Jo. Talk to me."

"No, I mean *really* talk. Before we go anywhere. Before you do this day-care thing. You're making a big mistake by—"

"Wait." The flash in his eyes silenced her. "Stay here." Crossing the riding ring, he spoke to Billy and Adela.

Jamming her hands into her pockets, she fought the urge to flee, unsure whether her heart raced from exasperation—or fear. She'd forgotten this was the man who didn't ask, who wielded money and persuasion to run his world. This was the man too much like Jason.

Trey tramped back, his expression darker than the clouds gathering overhead. The hand he wrapped around her arm made her stiffen in defense. If he was going to play power games, she couldn't let his nearness affect her, couldn't let his touch unravel her and make her yield.

But it did. She let him lead her into the stables, avoiding his harsh gaze. He stopped in the shadows and spun her to face him, his mouth set in a hard line that made the things she'd said about him to Adela seem terribly wrong. She'd never seen him so angry. She'd never felt so alone.

"All right, Jo. Billy's seen enough angry words. If you want to talk, talk here."

She looked vulnerable. Damn it, Jo looked almost afraid. Trey loosened his grip, let some of his frustration drain away as he considered the desolate amber of her eyes. He was acting like a Neanderthal, taking all his anger at himself out on her. Hadn't he known from the very beginning that she didn't approve of him? It was his own damn fault he hadn't stopped seeing her then.

He should let her go, just walk out of here and never see her again. But somehow it wasn't a matter of choice anymore. He couldn't leave, not until they had this out, not until he discovered what caused her shadows.

"All right, let's have it."

She hesitated. "It's Billy. Can't you see?" Her voice sounded almost pleading. Pulling herself up straight, she faced him squarely. "He doesn't want cowboy outfits and souvenirs. He doesn't want *things.*"

"But riding isn't—"

"He doesn't want ice-cream socials and riding parties."

She wasn't afraid anymore and she wasn't mad. Suddenly she looked so damn appealing, he almost wished she were. Anger was easier to fight.

"Trey, didn't your father ever spend time with you? Just *you?* Just being together and talking and making you feel like you were the most special person in the world?"

"I told you my father was..." Not the kind of person she was talking about. But Grandpa Shel was. With Grandpa Shel, he'd been Most Favorite Number One Grandson. He'd been special. He'd never felt that way with his father. He was still looking for acceptance from him.

"What are you remembering?" Jo asked quietly.

She must have read his face. "My grandfather."

"The compassionate Covington patriarch? The one who accepted Meira? The one you're named after."

Trey was the third Shelton Covington, all right, to his father's great dismay. Suddenly he remembered his mother sitting on the chaise where she spent so much of her last months. Playing checkers with Billy, cherishing his hugs, looking up at Trey over his unruly cowlicks and murmuring, *Remember you're a Covington.*

She hadn't meant his father at all.

But he'd been acting like his father. *And Jo didn't like him that way.*

"I knew you wouldn't like hearing this, Trey, but—"

"Jo McPherson, you have just made me a happy man."

The sweet round O of her lips was more than a man could be expected to resist, not when she looked so astonished. And so inviting. Pulling her into his arms, he kissed her, thoroughly, soundly, feeling a satisfied chuckle build in his chest.

So Jo didn't like a money-wielding controller who didn't know how to relate to his son. Well, it seemed they had something in common after all, because neither did he.

Jo was seething. She was absolutely incensed at the laughter rumbling in Trey's throat, irate that he was kissing her. Furious that she couldn't seem to resist. She wanted to shout at him. She wanted to run away. She wanted to stay in his arms... forever.

Pushing against his broad chest, she turned from his kiss. "Don't."

"Jo, what's the matter?"

"I thought you understood what I was saying, but you obviously weren't paying attention. Let me go."

Trey was trying to distract her, using compliments and kisses to throw her off, to get what he wanted. Just as Jason had. But she'd already learned that lesson. Pulling free from his grip, she started to run.

"Jo, wait—"

A crash of thunder slowed her steps. Through the open stable door she saw rain.

A storm. The realization jarred her more than the thunder had. "Trey, the kids!"

Boots pounding, he caught up with her as she dashed outside. The sky roiled with thunderheads, filling the air with the pungent scent of ozone, spewing rain in heavy drops that slammed into her like ice water. A jagged bolt of light slashed through the ominous gray, followed too soon by a thunderous crash that sent fear thrusting into her heart and coursing across her skin.

Lightning! They had to get the children in! Through the downpour she could see Rocinante thrashing at his reins tied to the hitching rail. The riding ring was empty.

Dear God. It was happening all over again. But this wasn't the nightmare returning to torment her sleep. This was here. This was real. Billy had run away—in a lightning-charged storm.

"I've got to get a horse. We've got to go after them." She whirled toward the stables.

"I'll get Rocinante."

Trey's voice faded into the rain, but she didn't look back. Her boots drummed on the hard stable floor as she raced in. "Kody, where are you? I need your help."

At her shout, he appeared in the doorway of the tack room, saddle soap and sponge in his hands.

"The children! They're gone. We have to go after them." She could feel her fright crescendo with her rising voice.

Following Kody into the tack room, she emerged with a saddle and pads. Kody was right behind her with the same. "Where's Trey?"

"Here." He dashed into the stables, boots pounding in counterpoint to Rocinante's hooves as he led the big stallion after him.

Jo headed down the aisle and into a stall.

"What happened?" Kody called over the increasing thrum of the rain.

His calm failed to quiet her quaking as she slid the saddle pad onto the horse's back. "We left Billy with Adela. We were gone only a few minutes. I can't believe no one saw them."

Trey squeezed into the stall, carrying dark green rain ponchos. "Billy's ridden in the rain before. He's a pretty independent little horseman." He helped her settle the saddle into place.

"Didn't you see his face, Trey? That's what I was trying to tell you. Billy ran away."

"Ran away? He wouldn't—"

"Adela probably led him out for a look at the back pasture," Kody offered. "She's a levelheaded kid. They'll be all right."

A flash of light turned the stall white. Jo steadied the agitated horse, bracing for thunder while Trey adjusted the cinch. The lights flickered, followed by an ominous crack that made the walls reverberate and shook her to the bone. "We've got to go."

"Ready." He tossed her a poncho and rushed out of the stall ahead of her, his stride eating up the length of the aisle to Rocinante. Kody and his horse followed. They pulled the ponchos over their heads and mounted, then directed the animals outside.

Jo urged her horse into a gallop toward the back pasture with Trey and Kody on either side, hardly aware of the cold rain that flew from the brim of her hat and slithered down her neck. Racing up the rise, she strained to see over its edge, searching through the downpour for two small figures on horseback. They reached the level pasture, and her heart sank. Through the deluge, there was no sign of the children.

"Look. The gate. It's closed. They haven't been gone long enough to go through here. They must have ridden in the other direction." Jo forced her horse into a turn.

"Taka knows another path." Kody's voice penetrated her fear even through the buffeting rain. "Follow me." He led them to the far side of the pasture, where a stand of willows rose from dense undergrowth along a shallow wash.

The sight of rushing water in the usually dry wash made her breathe in sharply. Suddenly everything threatened danger. "There may be flash floods!" The children wouldn't know what to do. "We've got to find them soon."

Kody led them through the rising water into a narrow opening in the brush. On the other side, he stopped. "You two search up north toward the foothills. I'll go south." He swung his horse away. "If you don't find them in half an hour, come back to the ranch and we'll get more help."

One glance at her watch and all the reassurances Kody and Trey had offered blew away like a gust of wind. The kids had been gone too long. Even if they were level-headed and independent, anything could happen to two children on horseback in a thunderstorm.

As if to punctuate her foreboding, lines of lightning crackled through the sky, followed by another explosion of thunder. Her horse reared, shrieking alarm. Clutching the reins, she struggled to keep him under control, and a new fear kicked her pulse higher. What if the children's horses had bolted?

"Jo!" Trey's voice carried over pounding hoofbeats. "Slow down. We have to do this methodically." He caught up, slowing Rocinante as she pulled back on her own mount.

He was right. She had to get a grip, couldn't let panic take over. She had to fight her own urge to run away.

"Let's ride in a zigzag. You scan that side and I'll watch over here. Look for Adela's red shirt."

Without preamble, Trey had taken charge. For once, his unrelenting self-assurance comforted her as nothing else could, gave her the control she needed to keep from urging the horse into a gallop. Driving down her fear, she scoured the land. Trey rode nearby.

"Jo, I've got to know something." Taut with worry, his words penetrated the pounding rain. "Why do you think Billy ran away?"

She turned long enough to see he'd taken her seriously. "Billy wanted time with you yesterday. You gave him ice cream. He wanted time with you today, and you invited *me*. Then you took me away, left him behind, left him with a *girl*." She couldn't help the accusation in her voice, as if she could convey to him all of Billy's hurt.

"I understand about yesterday, Jo, but Billy understood about today. He knew we needed a guide. He *wanted* you along."

"Trey, you don't know what he wanted. I've been there before. I know." All the old anguish pushed to the surface, threatening to mingle tears with the cold rain that etched down her cheeks.

"*What* do you know, Jo? *How* do you know?"

Through the slowing rain, she could hear his concern. She had to make him grasp what he was risking with Billy.

"I had a student. Danny Harcourt." She paused. Tried to swallow the tightness in her throat. "He was fourteen...had a lot of problems." Turning away, she searched the landscape for a bright red shirt. Everything looked gray. She made herself draw in a long breath.

"I didn't understand why he was so moody. He lived with his dad. His dad seemed like a caring person."

Trey didn't stop scanning the countryside, but his posture told her he listened as intensely as he watched.

"His dad asked me along on some of their activities. At first Danny seemed pleased. After a few times, I knew something was wrong."

Trey turned. Even his eyes looked gray. "He ran away?"

She focused on the rain dripping from the brim of his Stetson and tried not to think of how wet and cold the children must be.

"Not then. But he stopped going with us. Jason told me he was busy with other kids. He even paid for them to do things together. I thought it was good for Danny, that he was making friends."

"That's when he ran?"

"No." Desperately she squinted into a stand of trees but saw nothing. She couldn't put off telling Trey. "It was when Jason told Danny he'd go to boarding school after we were married."

"You were going to *marry* him?"

"He hadn't even asked."

Trey's sharp oath cut through the steady drizzle, offering her, in some strange way, understanding, solace, even comfort. He rode in charged silence, and she searched the countryside for the sight of rain-soaked children. For the courage to finish telling him.

"That's why you left teaching. Because you felt responsible." There was a harsh edge to his voice.

"I was responsible. I shouldn't have gone out with the parent of one of my students. I should have seen what would happen."

"So you left after Danny turned up."

Trey was trying to make the telling easier, but he didn't understand. Runaways weren't always stories with happy endings. He had to know that, had to know why they needed to hurry.

"Danny was never found."

* * *

Trey didn't even try to muffle the curse that exploded from his growing outrage. No wonder ghosts haunted Jo's eyes, no wonder she grieved. A kid was gone—possibly dead. She carried the heavy weight of self-blame.

"Jo, you can't believe you were responsible for Danny. You were probably the best thing that ever happened to him."

"I was his teacher. I used incredibly bad judgment."

The sorrow in her voice permeated him like the cold seeping through his wet clothes under the poncho.

"I don't want the same thing to happen to Billy." She reined her horse away toward a formation of rocks.

Suddenly he could see it all clearly. The kid—Danny—was the reason Jo shielded her heart from Billy. Danny's father was the reason she wanted nothing to do with *him*.

Spurring his horse forward, he caught up with her. "We'll find them, Jo. They'll be okay. I don't believe Billy ran, but we'll find out. You'll see—there's a simple explanation to all this, one that'll set your mind at ease."

Damn, he hoped he was right. Because if he wasn't . . . He tilted his face to clouds that looked as if they were thinning, felt the cold of intermittent drops on his cheeks. The rain was letting up, but that didn't stop the chill that swept through him as he scrutinized the barren rocks.

If he wasn't right? Maybe he *had* hurt Billy so much that he'd wanted to run. He'd have a lot of catching up to do, a lot of amends to make. He'd have to prove to Billy that he loved him. He'd have to convince Jo he wasn't like his father. He wasn't like Danny's father.

If he wasn't right? Images of runaway horses, of lightning and flash floods and lost children pushed into his mind, but he shoved them fiercely away. He couldn't let fear cloud his thinking, wouldn't even consider what *not* finding the children would do to him. What it would do to Jo.

"Trey, look. Over there." She pointed to a grove of cottonwoods at the foot of a small mesa.

Through the grayness of the still-falling drizzle, he squinted, trying to identify vague dark shapes. Horses. Two horses, standing together under cover of the trees. His sudden hope gave way to sharp fear as they rode near enough to see their reins dragging the wet earth. If anything had happened to Billy...

No. Clenching his jaw, he refused to dwell on the implications of empty saddles. Pulse hammering, he searched the surrounding terrain.

Behind the trees, low scrub and eroding rock rose to an overhang at the top of a bluff. "Jo, up there. Isn't that a cave?" Cupping his hands to his mouth, he shouted the children's names. Waiting, praying, he urged Rocinante forward.

From the shadows of the overhang, a small head appeared, followed by another—the most wet, bedraggled, wonderful little heads he'd ever seen.

"It's them!" Jo leapt from her horse and started to run.

Abandoning Rocinante, he raced after her, gaze riveted on the two children who waved and shouted from the rim above. He'd never heard such a marvelous garble of excitement, such glorious, wonderful noise. Never again would he object to Billy's chatter, because it meant he was okay, and happy. And *with* him. Thank God he and Adela were here.

"Daddy!" Billy ran to the edge to meet him.

Trey scrambled to the top and swept his wet little son into his arms, burying his face in his damp shoulder. He didn't care if the tears adding to the wetness were probably his own. His son was alive and in his arms.

Looking up, he saw Jo hugging the little girl.

Billy reached an arm out to them. "'Dela. Deputy Jo."

In one long stride, Trey closed the distance between them, and drew them into a hug, a circle of tears and laughter, of shared thanksgiving.

It was Jo who backed away first. "We've got to get your clothes dried before we head back."

He could almost feel her pull into herself, just as Billy had done this past year. Yanking his poncho over his head, he held it out to her.

"It looks like the rain's stopping. Get them out of those clothes and under the ponchos with you. I'll start a fire."

"Right."

She turned away, but not before he saw her swipe fingertips under her eyes. Wiping away tears—like his own. Tears that sprang from relief and gratitude, not from another tragedy that she might well have blamed on herself.

He should be glad for those tears, because they meant she still let herself care. The memory of two more lost children surely would have locked her heart away forever.

Chapter Eleven

Jenny fretted about Chaps while the widow Abigail told her and little Butch stories to keep their minds off the storm. She related how she'd worked in a dance hall when she was young and pretty, how she'd fallen in love with the most handsome cowboy that ever rode into Santa Feliz. Course, when it came to proposals of marriage, the local farmer had been the one to ask her. But her heart never forgot that rugged, winsome cowboy.

Miracles still happened. The children were okay. Jo had finally shared her ghosts.

Trey sought her gaze above the almost-dry heads of the two youngsters mounted on horses between them. Her tentative smile spoke volumes: overwhelming relief, heart-bursting thankfulness. And something he'd seen for the first time during the storm: a fragile vulnerability. But the shadows, at least for the moment, were gone.

He had so much to thank her for. But he hadn't told her, hadn't followed the urge to wrap her in his arms as he had the sodden, laughing children, to cherish her for the precious gifts she'd given him. But he would. Soon.

"Daddy, 'Dela told me cowboy stories. To keep me from being scared. I wasn't scared."

Trey's chest expanded with gratitude at the sound of his son's proud voice. "Is she a good storyteller?"

Billy nodded, tawny hair flopping into his eyes. "She learned from Deputy Jo."

"Deputy Jo's . . . the best." He wouldn't say teacher, wouldn't risk calling up those dark memories again. "She tells things so you pay attention." He smiled across at her, wanting to let her know he'd never forget the things she'd told him, from their confrontation in the barn to the terrible loss she'd experienced.

Instead of understanding, there were questions in her eyes, an urgency for the explanations she hadn't asked for since they'd found the children. She'd been as unwilling as he to spoil their joy, but he could see she wouldn't forgo the truth any longer.

"Adela, what happened?" Jo's voice was gentle.

Billy's head dipped.

"It's okay, Billy. It wasn't your fault." Adela reached to touch his arm, then looked up at Trey. "He was doing so good. He rode all the way to the end of the ring by himself. Then lightning scared Taka. I got on Dusty to catch them, but the thunder made them run away."

"The riding ring gate was open?"

Though Jo spoke the words mildly, Trey could hear guilt stalking her again.

Adela nodded. "Billy's dad . . . forgot to close it." She all but whispered, as if to protect him from blame.

But he wasn't the one who needed protecting. The questions in Jo's searching gaze tightened a knot in his chest. Honest error or culpable behavior? His...or hers?

"When we left, you were leading Taka. What happened?" Jo's voice held only concern—and lurking phantoms.

Adela's chin rose, her dark eyes unwavering as she looked to Trey. "Billy started to cry. He made Taka go faster. It was my fault. I lost hold of the reins."

"*I* was the one who left the gate open." Trey spoke quickly, looked squarely at Jo to drive the point home. "If there is *any* fault to be laid, it's mine."

Her eyes hardened with denial. "Why were you crying, Billy?"

"I didn't want Daddy to be mad at you," he murmured into his collar. "I didn't want you to fight."

Jo's swift intake of breath confirmed Trey's worst fear. She was blaming herself.

"Jo, you can't—" He saw her stiffen and retreat.

Jumping from her horse, she left a fleeting image of darkening amber-gold eyes. She wouldn't look at him as she swung the pasture gate open and motioned them through. All the way to the barn, she rode in silence, eyes straight ahead. Withdrawn once more into the company of ghosts.

He knew, with a certainty that left him seething, exactly what she was thinking. She'd convinced herself that Billy had run away. She really believed she'd been the reason, that she'd come between Billy and him. Just as she thought she had with Danny and his father. He and Billy reminded her too much of that terrible loss.

But damn it, she had no reason to blame herself. And Danny's father obviously hadn't helped her with her grief. Danny's father hadn't deserved a woman like Jo.

But *he* was different. He didn't want her to turn away.

At the barn, she worked with him to dismount the children, keeping her distance, still refusing to look at him. He lifted Billy down in time to see her hug Adela.

Billy inched over and tugged her sleeve. "Can I have one, too?"

She hesitated, and Trey understood the struggle in her eyes—the tenderness, the not-quite hidden urge to flee. The slow, sad smile. She knelt before Billy, let him wrap his arms around her neck and enveloped him with her own.

"Adela and Billy were very brave today," Trey offered, wondering at the ache in his chest as she clung to his son. "I'm proud of them both. And you, Jo."

She brushed fingers back through Billy's unruly cowlicks, then stood. Moisture glittered on her lashes. "Goodbye, Trey." Her eyes were wide and unblinking.

"Jo, wait."

But she was gone, her long legs consuming the distance to the barn. The ache in his chest sharpened as he watched her go. She'd given him a clear message, and it didn't mean *hasta mañana*, cowboy.

Her curt words pierced an emptiness inside him, a void he hadn't let himself admit. He'd almost grown used to it—until he met her. With Jo, he hadn't felt alone. He'd felt alive.

Damn.

Somewhere along the trail, he'd fallen in love with her.

Jo didn't see the sun break through the retreating clouds. Her blue minivan slowed to a stop in front of

Meira's place, and she let the engine idle, the key forgotten in the ignition. Resting her forehead against the steering wheel, she breathed a ragged sigh. Remembered rain and lightning. Saw only gray.

Thank God they'd found the children. If anything had happened... If they hadn't found them... The thoughts were too devastating to complete.

But she had to stop imagining the worst, just as she'd finally had to stop driving aimlessly. She had to make the morning's narrow escape serve a good purpose, and that was to come to her senses. She'd been a fool to let herself get involved.

After jerking out the key, she headed up the sidewalk, all but oblivious to the narrow street, the adobe house she'd come to love. Instead she worried about the woman who'd given her this refuge. Meira. Was she satisfied with what Trey was proposing? Would she be able to stand up against his father?

If she could be assured of that, then she could put Billy—and Trey—out of her life. Even if they'd still be in her heart.

At the front door, no New Age music floated out, no striped tabby appeared to wrap himself around her ankles. She knocked, praying Meira wasn't gone, desperate to get this over with so she could escape to her apartment and begin the forgetting all over again. This time, she had so much more to forget.

"I'm *com-ing*." Meira's voice pushed back the fringes of the gray. "Jo! I was hoping it was you." Coppery ringlets framed her smiling face. Swinging the noisy screen open, she beckoned Jo in.

"I have to talk to you. Is Trey's father coming to meet with you? He said you might sell—"

"Honey, you look like something Flannigan wouldn't even consider dragging in. Come to the kitchen. I have tea brewing."

Meira led her through the strands of amber beads hanging in the kitchen doorway, making them sway and click like the sound of seeds in a gourd.

"There's coffee, too. I made it for Trey, but there's more than enough."

Her heart wrenched as he shot up from where he sat hunched at the kitchen table. The chair scraped across the tiled floor.

"Where have you *been?*" He took a step toward her. Stopped. Gray-green eyes glowered darker than storm clouds, but all that brusqueness failed to hide a lightning flash of relief. "We need to talk."

"You mean *you* do." She shot back the words, fighting her own sudden gladness and the stumbling beat of her heart. "I want to know what you've talked Meira out of. I want proof you haven't promised her circuses and parades... and a band of camels playing seventy-six trombones."

His sun-tinged brows tilted at that, framing unwilling amusement. She hadn't meant to provoke that smile. Just another part of him she'd have to forget.

"I promised *you,* Jo, that whatever happens won't bring harm to Meira. If she doesn't want to be involved, I'll drop this whole thing. I've already told her that." The growl had all but gone from his voice, though his gaze held hers fast, as if intensity alone could convince her.

It wasn't easy to relax her defenses. "I want to believe you, Trey." She did. More than anything she wanted to believe he wasn't like Jason, that Trey could stop wielding power and money to control his world.

"If Meira's satisfied with your promise, then I'm...satisfied. I'll stop interfering. I just have to hear it from you, Meira. Then I'll go." She stepped back, but the room was too small to escape the force of Trey's presence.

Meira stayed her with a gentle hand. "Jo, there's something you should know. I am not Trey's aunt."

Jo swallowed a sigh. "I know. You were widowed before he was born." As always, Meira's intentions were kind, but hearing her side of the feud wouldn't make any difference.

"I didn't marry Cliff," Meira countered. "I never carried his child. Trey didn't know that until today."

That stopped Jo in midbreath. "I don't understand."

"Come sit, and I'll explain."

She shouldn't. She'd had enough of stories. But she couldn't just walk away from this woman who'd given her a refuge when she'd needed it so badly.

Unwillingly she let Meira direct her into a chair across from Trey. Even through her numbness, she could feel the impact of his gaze.

"I thought Cliff and I were friends." Meira resumed her story. "He invited me for Thanksgiving because I couldn't afford to go home. That was the wonderful week I fell in love...with his brother."

"You fell in love with Trey's *father?*"

"Instantly. Completely. Madly." Meira's face radiated the glow of memories.

"But then why...?"

"Shelton was eight years older. We agreed not to rush so I could stay in school. We wrote. He called. Oh, his phone bills must have been atrocious." She shook her head, her face soft with wonder. Just as quickly, she sobered.

"All of a sudden, I stopped hearing from him. Not one call, and all my letters came back. There was nothing but empty silence."

Her voice wavered, and Jo saw a shimmer of tears in her eyes. She reached for her hand, offering comfort in return for all Meira had given her. Trey's hand settled over Jo's, sending heat spiraling through her.

"That was the beginning of the feud?" she blurted, fighting the need to snatch her hand away.

"No. After I ran out of tears, I finally had to accept that, for Shelton at least, it was just an infatuation. I didn't know about Cliff's jealousy, or the lies he'd written to his family. Not until his father contacted me." Slowly she pulled her hand away, and turned to look out the window. "That's when I learned of Cliff's death in Vietnam."

Jo's throat tightened with sympathy. She slipped her own hand free, keeping the memory of Trey's touch. "Did Shelton come to you then?"

"No. He couldn't. He was about to be married."

"Oh, Meira." For Trey's father it *had* been just an infatuation. That damnable tycoon had been as heartless then as he was now. He was still causing Meira grief.

"It wasn't what you're thinking, Jo." There were no tears in Meira's voice now. "Shelton's father brought me a letter. Shelton wrote how devastated he'd been by what Cliff had written the family, how he'd finally resigned himself to losing me. In anguish, he'd proposed to Clara. The wedding was in two weeks.

"He said he simply couldn't bring more grief and embarrassment to his family by breaking the engagement. He had to do what was right.

"But he gave me a wonderful gift." Meira's voice caught. "He said I would always be his one and only love."

The words every woman hoped to hear. But how could words alone have salved Meira's loss? And what about the wife who spent her life never hearing them?

What about the son? Jo's gaze flew to Trey. How would he handle the long-held secret, a secret that surely would have broken his mother's heart?

But instead of anger, his face held quiet acceptance. "I think my mother must have known she wasn't my father's first love, Jo, but she adored him, and he was good to her. I believe she thought she had enough love for them both."

Meira tugged the corner of her bright blue smock to her eyes. "Jo, I am going to meet with Shelton. I may agree to sell my land." Though her voice quavered, her tone left no doubt about her determination.

"Are you sure that's wise?"

"I've learned a lot about wisdom, Jo. Like knowing when to follow your heart." Meira rose abruptly and moved to the stove. "Trey, take Jo somewhere and tell her the rest." Her usual commanding tone came out a bit soggy, which made her smile. "And get it right so she'll stop worrying about me."

Outside, Trey followed her along the lilac-lined path. The flowers were almost spent now, withered like dark purple memories, like the blooms that fell to her kitchen table from the bouquet Trey had picked for her.

Hurrying ahead, she sought the haven of her small courtyard. But the flowers there were bent and broken, and the paper bags of the *farolitos* had crumpled to wet lumps. Her refuge no longer offered comfort. Too late, she remembered the courtyard hadn't protected her from Trey's kiss.

Digging into her jeans, she found a cinnamon drop and slipped it into her mouth. "All right, Trey, finish Meira's story."

He settled onto the bench, one damp boot on the seat, and watched her. "Seems Grandpa Shel tried to talk Meira into going back with him to stop the wedding. If Meira hadn't refused, I might not be here today."

His coaxing smile tugged at her heart. She turned away and busied her unsteady fingers by plucking battered blossoms from rain-drenched flowers. What was she going to do with the sadness she felt for Meira? With the loneliness at the thought that this button-down cowboy was going to ride out of her life? Catching her bottom lip between her teeth, she moved farther away. "What about the land? The feud?"

"I guess there never was a feud. Meira said Grandpa Shel bought the land hoping it would bring her and my father back together someday. When that didn't work, he willed it to them—with the condition that neither could sell without the agreement of the other." He chuckled. "Guess he's finally going to get his way."

The deep laughter captured her heart all over again at the same time anxiety crept up her spine. Another Covington using money and control to get what he wanted—even from the grave. She shuddered.

"They'll be back together, but your father seems a lot more interested in raising camels than renewing a relationship. You told me yourself he uses land to make money. He's going to play on Meira's feelings and—"

"Jo?"

"...and rob her of another of her—"

"Jo."

She hadn't seen him get up, but he stood before her, so close she caught the scent of mesquite smoke from his fire-dried clothes. How could she let this happen again?

"Listen to me, Jo."

He clasped her shoulders, holding her with the calm of those deep forest green eyes, and she couldn't find the strength to flee.

"When Meira was there that Thanksgiving, they went to the zoo. They saw the camels there, and Meira told my father she'd always wanted to ride one.

"Before she went back to school, he made her a promise—the next time they were together, he'd find one for her to ride."

"Your father promised . . . ?" Suddenly his meaning became stunningly clear. "He still loves her," she whispered.

Sunlight sparkled in Trey's eyes. "I never would have thought the old boy capable of it, but I think he does, Jo. I think Meira still loves him, too."

The revelation was almost too much to absorb, especially with Trey holding her, with her heart pounding. But with it came a realization that left her stricken. "Then the camel ranch was just a ruse?"

He grinned. "More like a secret-code message. You see? You can stop worrying about Meira now."

She could. Meira's Seeds for Tomorrow farm and the man she'd fallen in love with . . . all of her dreams could come true now. There would be no camel ranch to intrude.

She searched Trey's eyes, dark green and inviting like the bed of a forest floor. Saw his delight shift to something certain and abiding. Desire. He was going to kiss her, and she couldn't stop him. Didn't want to stop him.

He gathered her into his arms as if he could catch up all the pain of the past, all the fears of the present, and kiss them away. His arms wrapped around her, shielding her from the memories of Jason's deception, from the grief of Danny's loss, from the fears she'd had for Meira and for Billy.

Lowering his mouth to hers, he drew in her breath, tasted her lips, cherished her with the sweet plunder of his tongue, wanted her with the taut hardness of his body.

His kisses drove away thoughts of everything but his rich taste of coffee and the pressure of his hand moving up her back to winnow into her hair. He sent ribbons of heat curling through her, making her weak, making her want. Sounds, like soft moans, hummed from him, sang from her, promising dreams... promising tomorrow...

Fighting for air and control and sanity, she splayed a hand on his chest. "No." The word was more plea than command.

"Hey." His voice was soft, and his forehead came to rest against hers. His fingers found her chin, nudged her gently. "I'm not the bad guy, remember?" His breath feathered her cheek. "There's something between us— you know there is, Jo. A woman doesn't kiss a man like that out of gratitude. Why won't you let it happen?"

Because she couldn't. Because she cared about him; she cared about Billy too much to come between them. And she would... always... no matter how much Trey denied it. Billy had made that frighteningly clear. The older he grew, the more he would.

She couldn't live with that. She couldn't live with the fear.

"Jo? There won't be any camels to gobble up Meira's crops."

Which meant no ranch, no rugged cowboy riding the range, fulfilling the dream of a young boy who hadn't fit in. No whimsical sloe-eyed beasts to bring laughter and fun to kids. To Billy. To her.

"You're an attractive man, Trey." She pushed back, keeping her head down. "You have a lot to offer some woman."

She felt his hand hesitate at her chin, then pull away, leaving cold where before there had been his coaxing warmth. Leaving her heart emptier than she'd ever thought possible.

"Wait a minute, Jo."

She couldn't stop now. Tugging from the hand that tightened on her arm, she turned toward her door, keeping her tears hidden.

"Go away, Trey. I'm not interested in a rich Eastern banker."

This couldn't be happening. Trey didn't want to believe what he was hearing. In Cheryn's eyes, he'd been too much like Grandpa Shel. Now, Jo was rejecting him for being like his *father*.

Remember you're a Covington. That's what his mother had told him, all right. Trouble was, he still wasn't sure what kind of a Covington he was. But he was damn tired of everyone telling him what kind he ought to be.

"Jo!" He caught her as she reached her door, slapped a hand on either side of the frame and watched her turn within the circle of his arms to meet his gaze. Heat still smoldered in her eyes, along with the glint of tears.

It hurt him to see her hurt, but her tears gave at least a measure of hope. She wouldn't cry if she didn't care, would she?

"Look, I've got a lot to sort out, I know. A lot of changes to make with Billy. You showed me that."

Her eyes slammed shut, as if by the weight of her frown, and she turned her face to the side, her chin angled upward.

"Damn it, Jo, don't turn away from me." He slid a palm along the taut line of her jaw, almost lost his purpose in her silky warmth. But he coaxed her gently to look at him.

"Kody told me they call you Guacamole because under that tough cover of yours, you're a real softy. But you know what? I think Cinnamon's a better nickname. 'Cause you're sweet..." With his thumb, he wiped away the moist path of a tear on her cheek. "And spicy..." His eyes drifted to where she nipped the corner of her bottom lip.

He felt her tremble, fought the impulse to toss his miserably inadequate words to the wind and simply kiss her into yielding, love her into acceptance. But he wouldn't do that.

"You're solid, Jo. So much stronger than you give yourself credit for."

I'm not, she mouthed, her eyes somewhere between defiance and entreaty.

God, he wanted to shake her. He wanted to hold her fair face between his hands and talk sense into that sweet, too responsible head. He just wanted to love her.

"Jo, you could handle a couple of cowpokes like Billy and me. You could teach us about this business called love."

At his words, fire flared in her eyes. She jerked free of his touch. "Love isn't a business, Trey, and I'm not a teacher. You'll have to pay someone else to tutor you."

Her expression darkened with rejection that hit him hard and low in the gut, like a punch he hadn't seen coming. She wasn't going to let herself care for him. She would let memories eclipse the golden light of those eyes, let the ghosts of Danny and his wealthy father stay to torment her. Let them keep her from risking love again.

He didn't know how to fight phantoms.

The frustration was harsh... and familiar. Slowly he let his hands fall to his sides. Stepped away.

"Maybe Kody was right." He put his finger to his mouth, then touched it to the lines tightened between her brows. "So tough on the outside." Tracing tenderly down her nose, he stopped at her lips, their softness making him ache. "So tender on the inside. And all mixed up...here." He threaded his fingers through the sun-dried hair at her temple. "Maybe we both need some tutoring from Meira."

Lowering his head, he kissed her once more, but this time gently, lingering on the fullness of her lips, telling her with that kiss what he couldn't with words—that he understood that she hadn't forgiven herself, that he knew she still didn't trust him. That he didn't want to say goodbye.

But if she couldn't accept him for who he was, this time he'd have to walk away.

Chapter Twelve

*Jenny knew she had to decide—run the Dry
Goods Store and spend the rest of her life
weighin' and measurin' and countin' out licorice drops, or risk openin' her heart to a cowpoke named Chaps and his pint-size son. The
widow Abigail already told her there was plenty
of room for bean sprouts and cows out there on
that land. But Jenny feared there wasn't room
for her in those rugged cowboy hearts.*

Jo's eyes felt as if she'd slept in a sandbox. But that, she
reminded herself, was because she'd hardly slept at all.
She'd spent most of the past three nights fighting sheets
and blankets. And tears. But she'd finally made a decision.

Hefting her sleeping bag and backpack, she lugged
them to the front room and set them beside the door. A
waft of chill air accosted her through the screen, accom-

panied by the early-morning chatter of birds. Like excited children at a party. A birthday party. That just stirred a whole new raft of guilt—and another threat of tears.

She would not cry! Instead she shoved the thoughts away and hurried to the bedroom for a heavier jacket. Nights were still cold on the trails, and she couldn't head out for a three-day weekend if she wasn't prepared.

Kody just had to take her shift at the stables on Saturday. As long as she could get out of here, as long as she didn't have to say goodbye, she'd get through this. By the time she came back, Billy's party at the day-care center would be over and he and his grandfather would be gone.

Just as Trey had gone, back to Vermont, to "take care of some long overdue business," he'd told Meira. The very same day he'd walked away from her at her door. He'd probably decided to take some of that tutoring from Meira and go back to where he came from, just as Meira had when she'd thought Shelton had rejected her.

Well, that was what she wanted, wasn't it: to have Trey out of her life? She yanked the jacket with the zip-in lining from a hanger and whirled out of the closet, stopping stone-still at the sound of a faint knock.

It was too early. A little boy shouldn't be up at the crack of dawn, even if it was his birthday.

The rapping sounded again, the same timid, persistent call she'd made herself answer every time she'd been home the past two days, because she couldn't bring herself not to. But this morning she'd meant to be gone.

Her feet dragged across the small living room. Opening the screen, she automatically looked down.

Billy's shy smile was barely visible under the brim of the angled gray hat. Thumbs hooked in his pockets, he slouched in a familiar stance, all his lean weight thrust on one short leg, casting his shoulders into a parallel tilt.

Jo couldn't help an affectionate grin. "Good morning, Deputy Bill. Happy birthday." For this little guy she always seemed to find a smile, even though seeing him was like reopening an old wound. This miniature cowboy, dressed in pearl-button shirt and hand-tooled boots, was too painful a reminder of the father he idolized. The man she'd fallen in love with.

"Look!" Billy flashed a toothy grin, revealing a gaping hole in the bottom row.

"You lost a tooth! On your birthday. I think that's good luck."

Suddenly he became serious. "Can I come in?"

She should tell him it was too early, that she didn't take visitors before coffee. But somehow she hadn't managed to send him away even once since Trey had left him behind with Meira.

"Okay." She breathed a silent sigh and let him in. "I'll bet you're wondering about your present. I'll go—"

"No." He turned from his wandering path toward the bowl of cinnamon drops on the rustic coffee table. "Not *now*. When you come to my party." His attention drifted back to the candy. "My dad's gonna be there. Can I have a hot candy 'cause I lost my tooth?"

So Trey *was* coming back. She'd hoped with all her heart he would show up, even if she didn't agree with the bash Billy's grandfather was throwing, which was to be even more expensive than Trey's canceled riding party at the stables. Whatever kind of showy celebration they came up with, Billy needed his dad here.

"I don't think hot candy is such a good idea before breakfast. Is your dad at Aunt Meira's?"

"I already had cereal. And *two* pieces of toast. He's at the found hotel. I got to eat there last night. Can I *please* have a hot candy, Jo?"

She half nodded, struggling to stop the downward spiral of her feelings. How could they possibly go any lower than bottom? Trey was at La Fonda and hadn't called, hadn't knocked on her door when he'd come to get Billy. But she hadn't wanted to see him, right? She had no reason to feel abandoned.

"Grandpa and I are gonna be cowboys at my party." Billy popped a candy into his mouth and continued to wander the small living room, stopping to examine a cactus on the window ledge. "Just like my dad and me." He reached a tentative finger to test the spines.

Jo sucked in a breath and bit her lip.

"Ouch! Those are pricky." The finger disappeared into his mouth, and he moved on to the basket of pinecones by the whitewashed adobe fireplace. "Meira's gonna be my cowgirl grandma. My dad said it's okay to have lots of grandmas."

She could almost feel the sharp prick of the cactus, but she wasn't prepared for the stab of yearning at his news. Meira and Shelton were going to marry? Would Meira finally experience the love she'd waited so long to share?

"Listen, Billy, it's mighty early, and I have to—"

"I know. Meira said come right back." He moved to the door, stopped at the pile of camping equipment and picked up the canvas-covered canteen, turning it over absently. "At home, my mom and dad and grandma and grandpa always came to my party." Head down, voice small, he sounded terribly young. "This time my mom won't be here." For a moment the corner of his hat tipped up as hesitant green eyes sought hers. "Will you be my cowgirl mom?"

She thought she'd mastered the tears, but new ones pushed at the corners of her eyes and gathered in her throat. This little boy who'd already wandered through every nook and cranny of her heart was threatening to take up permanent residence. And it hurt, it hurt so damn bad that she couldn't let him stay. But what could she tell him?

"Hey." Suddenly the canteen clanked to the floor. "Are you running away?" He sounded angry... and a little bit scared.

The question frightened *her*. "Running away? No. Why?"

"My dad says running away is when you take a bunch of your stuff—" he drew in a long breath "—and go away without telling anybody. I didn't want to run away. Taka ran away with *me*." He said the words defiantly, as if refusing to take the blame for a disobedient horse.

"Did your dad tell you that, too?"

"No, I thinked it by myself. Just like I thinked it's okay to have more than one mom."

It appeared Trey wasn't the only Covington who could cause her tears. Or make her smile.

"Bil-ly? Billy Covington, where are you?" Meira's singsong voice grew louder.

"I gotta go." He dashed out the screen door, letting it slam behind him. "See you at my party," he shouted.

"Now, Billy, remember what I told you." Meira's words carried on the crisp morning air. "Jo may not be able to come to your party. She has to do what she thinks is right."

Billy hadn't run away. After that indignant declaration, how could Jo have any doubts?

For a moment, just believing boosted her spirits, enough at least to get her moving. Grabbing up the canteen, she hurried to the small kitchen, the relief slipping with each step. Billy's revelation really didn't make a difference. Tears had been his way of protesting, this time. But what would happen when he became Danny's age? Teenagers knew so many more ways to make their anger heard.

Quickly she filled the water jug and returned to the living room where she snapped it to her backpack. Hoisting the bulging sack to one shoulder, she grabbed up the rest of the equipment and nudged the screen open.

It was time to leave. Time to get out on the road where things fell into perspective, up into the mountains where distance put things in their proper proportions. Where she could begin to forget.

For a moment, she stood, taking in the small apartment that had been her haven—the brightly tiled kitchen with the *ristras* of drying red peppers, the front room with the heavy wooden bench overflowing with pillows, the softly curved adobe fireplace and Meira's wonderful kachina painting hanging above.

But no little boy wandered around poking into things. And there was not one stick of furniture a lanky man could settle into. It wasn't a refuge anymore. It felt as lonely as an old abandoned town. Her heart was no longer here.

At the curb she shoved her equipment into the back of the van, jumped into the driver's seat and sped toward the highway. Shaded streets gave way to rolling hills and adobe homes peeking from emerald clusters of trees. But the sights didn't ease her restlessness any more than her apartment had.

Today all she could picture was a tall, lean cowboy with eyes like a forest in sunlight and tousled hair tipped in gold, with a smile that barely curled the corners of his straight mouth but found a place to dance in his eyes.

All she could think of was a birthday party for a little boy who looked just like him.

Tears threatened to fill the aching hollow in her chest. Two weeks ago Billy had barely looked her in the eye, yet in spite of the near tragedy at the stables, today he'd asked her to be his stand-in mom. Such swift acceptance was overwhelming. Humbling. More than she could handle.

At the intersection, she spun onto the familiar dirt road, sending dust and gravel flying as she pressed down on the accelerator. By the time Billy's party was under way she'd be well along the trails of the Sangre de Cristos, out of the picture until all the Covingtons returned to Vermont. She hadn't even told Meira where she was going.

That brought her foot off the accelerator, made her aware of the sudden heavy pulse in her veins. Slowly she let the van roll to a stop at the side of the road. She stared out at nothing, remembering the anger—and fear—that had clouded Billy's face.

By Billy's definition, she was running away.

She was a mature woman, not a wounded child. A capable person. A *teacher,* for God's sake.

But Billy had known.

She was running away.

From the Covington wealth and power? From Billy? Leaning forward, she switched off the key, slumped back into the seat. Felt cold where the sun couldn't reach.

She was running away from living.

It was true; it had been ever since she'd decided to come to Santa Fe. And it had almost worked. Until a make-believe cowboy had stepped right out of the stories she and Adela conjured up...and made her smile. Made her laugh again.

A caring man. Suddenly that seemed so clear. A man bent on honorable tasks no matter how hard she'd tried to see him as someone else.

And Billy? It was pretty apparent he'd known a lot of love. He adored his father, and he was willing to take on a new grandma. Even a stand-in mom. Willing to reach out to a spiny cactus of a world—and handle its wounds on his own.

She could learn a thing or two from him. Damn, she could learn a few dozen. She hadn't let herself reach out to him. Wouldn't touch the fire that flickered between her and his father.

She'd sent Trey away because she'd thought it was right. Just like Shelton Covington. But at least he'd been protecting someone else. She was denying her love because she was afraid.

Is that what she wanted? The kind of love that heated lonely nights with longing but never burned full strength? The kind of love she'd never recover from?

Meira said wisdom was knowing when to listen to her heart. But wisdom wasn't enough. She had to find the courage. To dream again, to reach out to Trey, to discover the strength of their fire. The courage to give her love.

She had to stop running away.

Bedlam. Shouts and giggles and clapping mingled with the melodic wheezes of a calliope, drawing Jo inexorably into the de Vargas Day-care Center. Organized chaos—that's what it was—a clown, balloons, puppets, a magic show, and everywhere children laughing. Everywhere, that whimsical dancing music.

But no sign of Trey.

How could her heart feel so vulnerable when she was surrounded by such happy pandemonium? Like an eighth-grader at her first school party, terrified that the boy she "liked" wouldn't be there, or that he wouldn't ask her to dance.

"Jo! I was afraid you were going to miss all this." Bonnie Carlson appeared from a gaggle of children and a forest of helium-filled balloons. "The de Vargas Daycare Center will never be the same. *I'll* never be the same." She grinned from ear to ear. "You'd better get in here. There've been a lot of people asking for you."

Bonnie's wink didn't ease her guilt. A lot of people? Probably Meira and Billy. Billy's invitation had been a precious gift, and she'd come so close to breaking his trust.

But she still had to face Trey, had to read in his eyes what she feared, that he and Billy were going back to their life in Vermont. That whatever had burned between them had ebbed, just as he'd let his boyish dreams fade.

"Where have you *been?*"

"Adela!" She hadn't expected her stable buddy to be here, especially not wearing a dress and having her dark hair braided with ribbons. "You look so pretty."

"You have to come see the puppet show. It's all about cowboys, and they even have a puppet named Chaps! And you have to meet Billy's grandpa. He's nice, but he's not as good a cowboy as Billy's daddy. But I think your landlady likes him." She giggled, dashing ahead of Jo into the big eating area where noisy children swarmed like ants watched over by laughing adults.

Her heart tripped at the sight of a tall man in a cowboy hat until she saw that he wasn't Trey but the man Trey might someday become. Less lean and solid, he looked as if he ate well and rode a desk chair hard, and the lines that carved the planes of his face spoke more of frowns than smiles.

With an unpracticed gesture, he lifted his natural straw Stetson to reveal perfectly combed white hair.

Meira turned from where she stood in front of him, her matching hat tilting back as she smiled up at him. He laid a hand on her shoulder, and the radiance in her face suddenly seemed to fill the room.

In that moment, all Jo's doubts disappeared. When Shelton Covington looked down at Meira, years fled from his face. He was a man deeply in love, and Meira was a glowing cowgirl grandma-to-be.

Adela managed to penetrate their cloud to bring them over, though they hardly looked away from each other until they reached Jo.

"Jo McPherson." Shelton held out a hand. "So you're the trail guide who looks after Meira's land."

"Mr. Covington." She returned his firm handshake and held his gaze in spite of the obvious appraisal in his brown eyes. "Guess I overreacted a little as a protector. I can see you and Meira have been able to work things out."

Her impetuous words stirred heat at her nape. The warmth moved upward as she watched his professional smile relax into a genuine grin.

"I think I'm going to like you, young lady. As a matter of fact, we *have* worked a few things out. I believe you're going to approve of the new arrangement."

"As long as Meira's happy—"

"Oh, I am, Jo. And I know a little boy who's delighted. Don't look now, but you're about to be—"

"Deputy Jo, you're late. Hi, Grandpa—hi, Meira."

Billy grabbed her hand and pulled. "Come *on!* You've got to come see Sally."

"Sally?"

"She's outside. You'll like her. My dad brought her special for the party."

Jo actually managed to smile. She actually let Billy drag her away while her hopes crashed and burned right there in that room.

She could stop looking for Trey now, because Billy was about to tow her straight to him—and the woman he'd brought back from Vermont.

"After you meet Sally we can light the cake. Grandpa said I have to share my birthday, so there's a candle for every kid. And a present, too."

Billy pushed through the back doors, dragging her after him, out into the bright sunlight.

"Jo! You're here."

Trey. She was glad to see him, glad to see the smile that warmed his eyes, even though her heart was shattering like a window struck by a flying rock. It hurt that bad.

Billy tugged her hand. "Come on, Jo, let's go see—"

"I need to talk to Jo now, son, remember? I'll bring her along in a minute."

Billy tilted his head to look up at her. "Aw right." Yanking her sleeve, he drew her down to his level, cupped his hands around her ear and whispered, "Please say yes." Then he dashed away.

Suddenly all her fragile new courage fled. Trey was going to make a speech. He was going to thank her for helping him with Billy and Meira and his dad, so now he could get on with his banking life. He was going to say goodbye and could Billy come visit her whenever his father and Meira came back to check on their land. She'd be the Aunt Jo that Billy came to visit with his grandfather. And she'd be alone. Just like Meira had been. Because she'd let him go.

"Walk with me a minute?" Trey slipped off his hat and rasped the brim between thumb and forefinger, his smile suddenly gone, his eyes full of appeal.

She had no defense against that kind of request. Falling into step beside him, she heard the gaiety of the play area fade as he led her to the side of the building.

"I was afraid you weren't coming." He stopped beside a huge old cottonwood tree, still worrying at his hat. Searching her face.

Making her melt without even touching her. "Billy asked me to come. I finally realized I couldn't let him down. I had to stop running."

That made his fingers stop, made something flash in his eyes that looked strangely like hope.

"I have something to tell you, Jo. I'd hoped it would let you stop running, but I should have known you'd get that done by yourself."

Something like fear mixed with hope stayed her breathing. "I don't understand."

"I made some contacts in Denver. Danny Harcourt isn't missing anymore. He's living with his grandmother."

For a moment, she thought she might faint, but Trey caught her arms, his hat forgotten as it fell to the ground. His hands felt strong and protective and made her want to fold herself into him, to reach out for the fire that had ignited between them and discover its full strength. She wanted to love him.

"Hey, Cinnamon, you okay?" For an instant, he touched her chin, and she thought her knees might buckle.

Instead she straightened, nodding. "Danny's okay? He's not...?" She couldn't even finish the thought.

"He's fine. He faxed me this. Asked me to give it to you." Trey pulled an envelope from his back pocket.

With trembling hands she opened it and read the message. Danny was going to high school in his grandmother's town. He saw his father once a month. He was doing well. He was thinking about becoming a teacher... like her.

"Oh, Trey." Tears welled and she didn't fight them. Tears for the wonderful gift he'd given her. Tears for the love she couldn't give him. "Thank you," she whispered.

She turned, but he caught her and pulled her back, held her with hands that made her yearn, with a look so entreating she wondered how she could ever have compared him to Jason.

"Now it's my turn to thank you."

"You don't have anything to thank me for."

"But I do. Remember when you asked about my dreams...the square-peg dreams of a misfit Eastern kid? You told me to go after them, Jo. You sent me away, and I didn't want to go. But this song came on the radio. Billy Ray was singing about dreams that move on when you wait too long, and he was singing right to me.

"So I went back to Vermont, and I got me a dream."

"Trey, I'm..." What could she say? That she was glad he'd gone away, that he'd found another woman?

"I want you to come see." Scooping up his hat, he plopped it on his head, clasped her hand and led her back toward the play area. "I want you to meet Sally."

Was it courage or sheer cowardice that made her follow him to this dreadful encounter? She knew only that his hand was too firm and warm, his face too full of anticipation. Her heart wouldn't let go.

He pulled her through the crowd gathered under the trees near the colorful old Conestoga wagon, right up to the side of a fuzzy, brown-eyed, six-foot-tall, camel-colored...*camel!* Seated in the saddle on its one-humped back was a leery, excited Billy, holding on for dear life.

Trey grasped the bright red bridle and pulled Sally's pouty muzzle down to Jo's eye level. "Jo, meet Sally."

Reflex made her cringe as Sally gave her a soulful look and leaned nearer to sniff her hair. But she couldn't hold back a delighted laugh.

"I think she likes you. She only takes to people I recommend."

He handed the animal back and drew Jo away, around the wagon and out of sight of Sally and her admirers. There in the shade of the giant trees, suddenly he wasn't moving away anymore. He was closing in on her like a cowboy after a skittish calf. The intent in his eyes made her shiver with anticipation, and she didn't realize she was backing up until she felt the hard wood of a wagon wheel at her back.

"Um, so what are you going to do with one mangy camel?" It wasn't easy to keep her composure when he raised his hand to the back of her neck. Ripples of anticipation skimmed across her skin in every direction.

"First off, there's going to be a wedding." His fingers spread into her hair, making her tingle.

"A wedding?" she managed to ask, searching for strength to resist him. Finding none.

"Sally's beau, Henry, is waiting for her out on my land. They're real anxious to get a family started." His thumb stroked her cheekbone.

"Your...land?"

"Mmm." His mouth brushed hers, and tugged gently at her bottom lip, sending rivers of desire coursing through her.

She let her hands find his chest, and he pulled back just enough to look at her. In that instant, she knew she'd fallen in love with these smiling green eyes the very first time she'd seen him.

"Meira drove a helluva lot harder bargain than Dad. You'd have been proud of her." He kissed her lightly on the nose. "But they finally agreed. Does Covington Camel Ranch sound too formal for Santa Fe?"

"They sold *you* their land?"

"Only on the condition that I keep a little plot for gardening. And flowers. I was thinking of impatiens and geraniums, maybe a goat flowerpot or two...and a whole lot of lilac bushes."

There were so many things Trey wasn't saying, so many things she didn't know how to say. "What about Billy?"

"Billy loves his mom, Jo, but he loves you, too. He told me. I think we can work it out, if you'll give us a chance." He bent to kiss her lightly, invitingly. "Billy also told me he didn't think love could be counted."

Not something that could be measured. But when you loved someone, that meant you could be counted on. Forever. Like Meira and Shelton.

She had to be willing to be counted on, no matter what. Really loving meant being willing to risk.

Trey slid his other hand to cover hers on his chest. "I don't think Sally and Henry would mind a double wedding. What do you think?"

What she thought was that it was about time she took that risk. "I think Billy's too young to get married."

He stepped back at that, his brows escalating over eyes that danced with mischief, his mouth broadening into the widest grin she'd ever seen. "Then I guess I'll just have to marry you myself." He lowered his mouth to hers, kissing her deeply.

What she thought was that her heart would never stop singing.

"I love you, Jo, but I don't intend to wait a lifetime like Dad and Meira did. You'd better say yes, because I won't let you let me go."

Trey Covington was a man who decided what he wanted and went after it. And she wasn't afraid anymore. "I love you, Trey. And I love Billy. I might even learn a certain fondness for Sally."

"Come 'ere, Cinnamon."

He enfolded her in his arms, and the love in that smile before he kissed her promised she'd never want to run away again.

So Chaps handed the reins to his son and leaned to kiss his new bride, Jenny. The team of eight fine camels pulled that handsome Conestoga wagon right off into the glorious New Mexico sunset. Together they'd travel badlands and happy trails with all the love in the world to see them through.

And they all lived happily ever after. The end.

* * * * *

COMING NEXT MONTH

#1114 DADDY ON BOARD—Terry Essig
Fabulous Fathers

Lenore Pettit's son needed a father figure, and he picked her boss, Paul McDaniels. For Tim's sake she agreed to a vacation with Paul and his daughter. But they could never be a family—could they?

#1115 THE COWBOY AND THE PRINCESS—
Lindsay Longford

Hank Tyler had nothing to offer a woman—he'd given up his heart long ago. And "princess" Gillian Elliott would certainly not be the exception. But Hank couldn't resist finding out if under the "princess" image lay a sweet and loving lady....

#1116 ALONG COMES BABY—Anne Peters
First Comes Marriage

When Ben Kertin found a pregnant woman hiding on his ranch he couldn't turn her away. Marcie Hillier needed protection, and marriage seemed the best solution. Until Ben began wishing for more than a temporary arrangement....

#1117 WILD WEST WIFE—Jayne Addison

Josh Spencer would never allow a woman to mess with his Wild West ranch! He was determined to show Carly Gerard, his new partner, that rodeos were not for city slickers. Until Josh began thinking of Carly in very wifely terms.

#1118 FORTUNE'S BRIDE—Donna Clayton

Dylan Mitchell had sworn off romance for life; he could take care of himself and his young daughter without anyone's help. Then Laura Adams inherited part of his company, and Dylan found himself falling for this bride of fortune!

#1119 SECOND CHANCE FAMILY—Laura Anthony

Single mom Savannah Markum needed help against cattle rustlers, but she hadn't counted on the inspector being her ex-fiancé, Matt Forrester. Savannah had vowed never to marry a lawman, but seeing Matt again made her wonder if their love deserved a second chance.

Take 4 bestselling love stories FREE

Plus get a FREE surprise gift!

Silhouette

SPECIAL EDITION ™

CELEBRATION 1000

It's our 1000th Special Edition and we're celebrating!

Join us for some wonderful stories in a special
celebration with some of your favorite authors!
And starting the celebration is

Diana Palmer
with
MAGGIE'S DAD
(SE #991, November)

Returning home, Antonia Hayes was determined
not to fall again for Powell Long. But the single dad
was sexier than ever—and he had *definite* ideas
about their reunion!

Celebration 1000! kicks off in the month
of November—don't miss it! Watch for books
by Lindsay McKenna, Jennifer Mikels,
Celeste Hamilton, Christine Flynn and
Brittany Young. You'll fall in love with our
next 1000 special stories!

Tall, dark and...dangerous...

Strangers in the Night

Just in time for the exciting Halloween season,
Silhouette brings you three spooky love stories in this
fabulous collection. You will love these original stories
that combine sensual romance with just a taste of
danger. Brought to you by these fabulous authors:

Anne Stuart

Chelsea Quinn Yarbro

Maggie Shayne

Available in October at a store near you.

Only from

Silhouette®

—where passion lives.

Become a Privileged Woman,
You'll be entitled to all these Free Benefits. And Free Gifts, too.

To thank you for buying our books, we've designed an exclusive FREE program called *PAGES & PRIVILEGES™*. You can enroll with just one Proof of Purchase, and get the kind of luxuries that, until now, you could only read about.

BIG HOTEL DISCOUNTS

A privileged woman stays in the finest hotels. And so can you—at up to 60% off! Imagine standing in a hotel check-in line and watching as the guest in front of you pays $150 for the same room that's only costing you $60. Your *Pages & Privileges* discounts are good at Sheraton, Marriott, Best Western, Hyatt and thousands of other fine hotels all over the U.S., Canada and Europe.

FREE DISCOUNT TRAVEL SERVICE

A privileged woman is always jetting to romantic places.

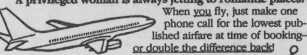

When you fly, just make one phone call for the lowest published airfare at time of booking— or double the difference back!

PLUS—you'll get a $25 voucher to use the first time you book a flight AND 5% cash back on every ticket you buy thereafter through the travel service!